Phantom of the Blockade

Phantom of the
Blockade

Stephen W. Meader

ILLUSTRATED BY VICTOR MAYS

ISBN 978-1-931177-16-0 cloth
ISBN 978-1-931177-17-7 paperback

SOUTHERN SKIES

LITTLE ROCK, ARKANSAS

www.southernskies.com

Foreword

The American Civil War, fought a hundred years ago, still stirs the memories and feelings of millions. Some say it was an unnecessary war, others that it was inevitable. But it demonstrated one thing—the courage of Americans, rich and poor, North and South. It proved for all time the fact that we are one nation, indivisible. And it put an end to the institution of slavery.

This story takes place in the final year of the long struggle. The inexperienced youngsters who marched out so gaily in '61, smart in their new uniforms, with bands playing and pretty girls cheering, were long since gone. Thousands had been killed or wounded or taken prisoners. Other thousands had turned into hard-bitten veterans, able to march all night, ragged and hungry, and fight a battle at dawn.

Half a dozen times in those years, the tides of fortune for both sides had risen high—the war almost won. Then by some mischance victory had slipped through their fingers. The Confederate armies were nearly always outmanned. But fine generalship and stubborn determination had kept them in the fight.

The superiority of the North in manpower, supplies, and food grew greater every day after the slaughter at Gettysburg. Yet the men in gray had a spirit that wouldn't give up. They tightened their belts and fought on, trusting in such great commanders as their beloved Lee.

One of the things that kept the Confederate cause alive far longer than might have been expected was the daring of the blockade runners. With most Southern ports sealed tight or in enemy hands, the little gray steamers dashed in and out of Wilmington, North Carolina, through cordons of Federal gunboats.

Unarmed and depending wholly on speed and deception, they carried cotton to Nassau or Bermuda to maintain Southern credit. And they brought back guns, ammunition, food, and medicine for the troops. The dangers were great, but the pay was high, and plenty of fine seamen were willing to take the risk.

The feats of the blockade runners described in this book were duplicated many times by actual ships. Their exploits and escapes form one of the least known but most thrilling chapters in the history of the War Between the States.

S. W. M.

Phantom of the Blockade

One

It was sunset when Anse O'Neal went aboard, carrying his duffel bag on his shoulder. The *Sea Sprite* lay low in the water. In double tiers on her deck, the cotton was stacked —three hundred bales of it—in addition to an even larger amount stowed in the hold. She would be drawing a full eight feet of water tonight, and they'd need a high tide to get over the bar.

Below decks, Anse could hear sounds of shoveling in the engine room, where the stokers were getting up steam. He moved on through the narrow passage between bales of cotton. Just forward of the paddle boxes was the wheel, and there he found the pilot, Hobe Gaskill. Hobe was an Ocracoker from the Outer Banks, like himself. He knew every shoal and channel on the treacherous North Carolina coast and was regarded as a top pilot among the blockade runners out of Wilmington.

"Howdy, Anse," he greeted the young seaman. "All set for another run?"

"Reckon I'm ready," Anse told him. "This is my sixth trip, so I'm beginnin' to get used to it. Don't feel quite as scared as I did at the start."

Gaskill grinned. "Runnin' skeert is part of the job," he replied. "I've been at it years, an' I still don't feel easy in my stummick till we're clear o' the last gunboat. But that's why they pay us good money."

"Where's the skipper?" Anse asked.

"Roundin' up the rest o' the crew, I reckon—an' maybe gittin' the latest news in town. Don't worry. He'll be aboard in plenty o' time. With a good dark night an' a flood tide at eleven, ye couldn't keep him ashore. He'll want to be well down the river by nine-thirty."

Anse stowed his gear under his bunk in the cramped little forecastle. There wasn't much that he owned—a spare set of dungarees, a couple of changes of underwear, and a dog-eared book on navigation. His savings were something else again. In the heavy money belt around his middle, he carried nearly a thousand dollars in gold. As Hobe said, sailors who ran the blockade were the best-paid seamen in the world. An ordinary deckhand could make better than two hundred dollars for a round trip—if he lived. And the wages weren't paid in Confederate paper money but in British pounds at Bermuda or Nassau.

Anse sat on the edge of his bunk and pinched himself to make sure he wasn't dreaming. It was hard to believe that a poor boy from the Outer Banks, barely turned seventeen, could have amassed such a fortune.

A tramp of feet outside announced the arrival of the rest of the crew. They came tumbling through the companionway, and a moment later the crisp commands of the captain were heard.

"All hands on deck!" he ordered. "Cast off and make sail."

The mooring lines were flung on deck, and the men sprang to the halyards. In a moment the two triangular sails were run up fore and aft. Forward, both jibs were set. With a light northwesterly breeze over the quarter and the engines at half speed, the *Sea Sprite* slipped down the Cape Fear River in the gathering dusk.

Like most of the steamers of her day, she was a side-wheeler. But her slim lines gave her extra speed. Nearly

two hundred feet long, she had a beam of only twenty feet, and her raked masts and stacks offered little resistance to the wind. From her tapered bow a light steel turtleback ran aft forty feet to protect the foredeck from spray. Even her paddle boxes had a teardrop design.

Amidships were the boilers, coal bunkers, and a pair of tough Glasgow-built engines that could send her along at race-horse speed. Almost as important as the captain of a blockade runner was the engineer. The *Sea Sprite* was lucky to have an unusual man in her engine room. Sandy MacIvor was a grizzled old Scotsman who could coax more steam from his boilers than any other engineer along the coast. He had been with the ship ever since she was launched in the Firth of Clyde.

Once the canvas was drawing, Anse took his station abaft the binnacle, where he could lend a hand at the wheel if called upon. He was near enough to overhear some of the talk between the skipper and pilot.

Captain Ransome Tracy was the boy's idol. His figure was lithe and powerful, and his gray uniform fitted him without a flaw. A daredevil young Charleston gentleman with a liking for ships, he had outfitted and sailed a privateer in the days just after Fort Sumter fell. Then, as the South's need for arms and supplies became more urgent, he took command of a blockade runner. Gradually the Federal net around Charleston had tightened. After the forts at Port Royal were taken by the Yankees, Charleston was cut off. Wilmington, North Carolina, became the one Atlantic port where runners could carry on their dangerous trade. It was there that he made his headquarters.

Tracy had soon become a legend along the coast. Twice he had made his escape after having ships sunk under him. A dozen times he had survived hair-raising encounters with the blockading fleet and brought his cargo safely to port. President Jefferson Davis himself had said that the Confederacy owed more to this daring young captain than to any other single civilian.

Tracy was frowning now as he watched the dark shore slip past. "Bad news in the city today," he told the pilot. "Hood's been beaten at Atlanta. Sherman's troops are probably burning the city right now. They say he packed all the people out of town first, though."

Gaskill shook his head. "Don't seem like we've had any real good news for quite a spell, sir," he growled. "Our boys still hangin' on at Petersburg?"

"Yes, things are all right there. Rations are running pretty short in Petersburg and Richmond, I'm told, but if we get through, we'll bring back supplies—bacon and coffee. The best thing I see ahead is the election in the North. The Democrats have nominated McClellan for president, and once Lincoln's out of office, they'll try to make peace. From all I hear, most of the folks up there are just as sick of the war as we are."

"That'll put us out of a job, sir!" Gaskill chuckled. "But the quicker it comes, the better for all of us. Ain't any sense in gettin' a lot more soldiers killed."

Tracy smiled and squared his shoulders. "O'Neal!" he ordered. "Take a pike and search the deck cotton. We'll be off Smithville in another hour."

Anse hastened to obey. He knew what the captain meant. Several times, on previous voyages, they had found stowaways hiding among the bales—Negro slaves trying to escape or deserters from the Confederate garrison at Wilmington. The boy seized a long, sharp pole from the rack and began prodding it into crevices between the bales of cotton. Methodically he moved up one side of the ship and down the other.

"Nobody hid, sir," he announced when he had completed the rounds. "Nothin' bigger'n a rat, anyhow."

"Very well," Tracy answered. "Get ready to lower a boat. I want you to get the latest word on what we'll find outside."

The steamer was coming into the wind, preparing to heave to. Anse called two other seamen and sprang to the davits. In a moment they had the dinghy over the side and were pulling for the shore, two hundred yards away.

Before the war, Smithville had been a fishing village and a hangout for the harbor pilots who took incoming ships up the river. Now it had a small force of militiamen manning the batteries below the town. They kept a constant vigil from the neck of land west of Fort Caswell and watched the movements of the Yankee blockaders.

The small boat made fast to a rickety pier. In the darkness Anse picked his way up the path to the tavern and through a haze of tobacco smoke to the bar. Half a dozen soldiers eyed him over their beer.

"I'm from the *Sea Sprite,* Cap'n Tracy," he explained quietly to the innkeeper. "We're ready to go out. What's it look like beyond the inlet?"

"Tain't good," the man replied, wiping his hands on his apron. "Take a calm night like this, an' they're all layin' out there below Smith's Island. Last I heard there was more'n a dozen of 'em jammed together so thick they're 'most touchin'."

"That's right," one of the militiamen put in. "I jest come off lookout, an' I reckon even a shark couldn't git through."

Anse thanked them and went back to the boat. The rowers bent to the oars, and a few minutes later they were alongside the blockade runner once more. When Anse gave his report, the captain merely nodded.

"Thought so," he said. "We'll try New Inlet."

The sails had already been run down, and the ship lay there dark in the gloom. Painted a neutral shade of gray-blue and without a light showing, she was almost invisible at night or in the mist. Now the skipper called for full speed ahead, and Gaskill swung her nose to port. Swiftly they cut across the broad river mouth toward the headland where the bastions of Fort Fisher loomed grim against the stars.

Hobe Gaskill turned the wheel over to Anse as they approached the inlet. "I'll keep a lookout," he said, "an' tell ye how to steer."

Nimbly the pilot sprang up on the starboard paddle box, where he had an unimpeded view forward. Captain Tracy, meanwhile, had climbed to the foremast crow's nest with a pair of night glasses in his hand. It was close to twelve o'clock. The tide had turned and was running out past Sheep's Head Rock like a millrace.

"Starboard yer helm two points," Gaskill called, and Anse gave the spokes a turn, swinging the bow to port.

"Now—steady as you go. The bar lies right ahead."

Above the cotton bales, Anse could see the pale line of breakers in the ship's path. He held fast to the wheel and felt the tremor of the speeding hull under the grating on which he stood. The paddles slapped spray as they moved into the surf. For one frightening moment the keel scraped bottom and the *Sea Sprite* seemed to hesitate. Then they were over, picking up speed again.

"Too big a load o' cotton," Gaskill grumbled as he came down and took the helm. "An hour later an' we'd ha' been aground."

Anse hurried forward, where he could peer into the darkness. As he reached the foremast, Tracy was descending the ratlines.

"Go aloft and take the lookout," the captain told him. "If you see anything, keep your voice down. I'm going to cut the engines to half speed."

The stumpy mast reached only forty feet above the deck, but from the crosstrees there was a good view of the sea around them. Very little wind was blowing. The sharp prow of the blockade runner knifed through the long ground swell with hardly a ripple. Suddenly Anse spotted a dim dot of light off the starboard bow. He waited to be sure, then called quietly to the deck.

"Gunboat about a mile ahead an' to starboard," he told the skipper. "She's movin' north across our course."

The engines slowed still more, and the *Sea Sprite* glided forward, silent except for the soft, rhythmic slap of the paddles.

Anse shivered a little in the chill night air. His eyes followed the lights of the Federal gunboat as she moved slowly northward and to port. She was still less than half a mile away when the *Sea Sprite* slipped across her wake.

Tracy came part way up the ratlines. "Any more in sight?" he asked.

"No, sir," said Anse. "All clear as far as I can see."

The captain went down, and ten seconds later the engines picked up speed. With the paddles thrashing louder, the trim little ship plowed eastward toward the Gulf Stream. If more blockaders had been accompanying the first one, they were soon left well astern.

Nobody did any sleeping on a blockade runner the first night out. Anse stayed at his lookout post for four more hours, and dawn was breaking when he climbed stiffly down. There was hot coffee waiting in the galley, and the cook was frying eggs to go with the country sausages he had laid in ashore. The crew of the *Sea Sprite* ate well.

Before he went to his bunk, Anse took a look at the bright morning. Back home on the sandy island where he had grown up, he knew the fishing boats would be going out with hopes of a good day's catch. Ocracoke seemed a long way from the war.

In the summer of 1861, there had been some excitement along the Banks. That was when Union forces had taken Hatteras and destroyed little Fort Morgan, in Ocracoke Inlet. But most of the island people simply wanted to be left alone. They owned no slaves and had no close ties with the Confederate mainland. Many of the men had worked for the Federal Government, building and tending lighthouses, and it was natural that they found little sympathy for the Southern cause. Just staying alive on the Outer Banks was hard enough without going off to fight in strange places, far from the sea.

Hobe Gaskill's case was somewhat different. He had never been content with fishing for a livelihood, and before the war he had fitted out a broad-beamed twenty-foot sloop for trading up and down the coast. Even after the Yankee blockade started, small craft usually went unmolested, and he had been able to navigate through the sounds, carrying salt fish and merchandise to some of the little towns where there were no Federal troops.

Then, in the summer of 1862, he visited the port of Wilmington. Pilots who knew the inlets were in great demand for running the blockade, and Hobe was offered astonishing wages to sail aboard the *Sea Sprite*. He brought his sloop, the *Goose*, back to Ocracoke and spent a few days there settling his affairs.

Anse was just over fifteen at the time. He was big for his age, long-legged and muscular, and he had been sailing boats since he was ten. When Gaskill offered him the sloop, Anse finally persuaded his father to let him handle her. And so had begun a new chapter in his life.

There wasn't much money to be made in the *Goose*, but it was a living and far more challenging than merely running nets in Pamlico Sound. He had one man for a crew—a free Negro named Joby, who had been Hobe Gaskill's helper and knew most of the channels.

Their trips took them to lonely fishing hamlets and a few larger towns along the shore. Usually they carried fish or oysters, yams, and other produce. For a few pennies they took letters from one port to another. Sometimes there were newspapers to deliver. But everywhere they went, they were sure of a welcome from people cut off from the rest of the world.

For a year and a half things went well with Anse. The *Goose* was known in the sounds, and the few Yankee patrols gave him no trouble. Then, in the time of February storms, he took the sloop out through Bogue Inlet, trying to make a short cut to Snead's Ferry. Night caught them just outside the New River bar, and the wind was rising. Joby thought he could find the channel, but somehow, in the darkness, he miscalculated. The sloop ran hard aground on a sandbank. They clung there shivering in the wind and spray till next morning, hoping to get her off at the next high tide.

But at dawn disaster came. A Yankee gunboat hove in sight, spotted the stranded vessel, and began firing. The two of them went over the side and swam ashore through the surf. From the dunes, they watched in helpless fury while the blockader pounded the poor old *Goose* to pieces with round shot.

That was when Anse turned Rebel. After two hungry

days of hiking through sand and marsh and woods, he managed to reach Wilmington. Joby had stayed behind, afraid of what the Confederates might do to him.

For several weeks the young Ocracoker lived by working as a roustabout on the docks, the only white man in a swarm of cheerful Negroes. He loaded cotton for his meals and slept among the bales. Then one morning the *Sea Sprite* came steaming up the river. Hobe Gaskill saw him at once from the deck and hurried down the gangplank to greet him. An hour later, when the pilot had given Tracy an exaggerated account of Anse's prowess as a seaman, the jaunty skipper had laughed and agreed to sign him on. After mailing a letter to his parents, he had sailed aboard the runner through the spring and summer.

Two

All morning a vigilant watch was kept, for there was always the chance of encountering a Yankee cruiser on patrol in the Gulf Stream. But neither smoke nor the white glint of topsails broke the clean line of the horizon. The day was perfect, with bright sun and balmy weather. They steamed through waters of a lovely blue under a cloudless sky. When Anse went to take his trick at the wheel, he was surprised to see a scowl on the pilot's face.

"Too durn' easy," Gaskill grumbled. "Don't like it when everything goes so smooth. I'd wager a week's pay we're headin' for trouble, an' I wouldn't wonder if it came before night."

Anse had too much respect for his friend's judgment to laugh at him, but it was hard to believe such a fine morning could be an omen of evil.

At noon the captain took a sight with the sextant and found they had made a hundred and thirty miles of easting since leaving New Inlet. Then he left the deck to the mate, a lanky South Carolinian named Calhoun, and went to his comfortable cabin aft. Anse, meanwhile, had snatched a couple of hours of sleep and was back on duty. There were no regular watches aboard a blockade runner. The men took catnaps when they could, always alert for a call.

In order to save coal, the engines were stopped and the

sails set. MacIvor banked his fires but kept a head of steam in the boilers so that power would be ready in any emergency. The breeze freshened from the northwest. The ship footed surprisingly well under the small amount of canvas she carried, and when Anse went aft to heave the log, he was able to report a speed of better than six knots.

The coal-grimed stokers came up on deck that afternoon, glad of a chance to loaf and enjoy the fresh air. There were eight of them—four Bahamian Negroes, three Portuguese from the Azores, and a burly savage who claimed to be a Seminole Indian. In a few minutes most of them had lines over the side, and they began hauling in an occasional small fish.

The men of the deck watch had no time for fishing. At the mate's orders they were continually trimming sail to get the best speed out of each shift in the wind. Every hour or two the lookout was changed at the foretop.

Anse had the wheel at four o'clock of the second day out when the man in the crow's nest reported a heavy haze to the east.

"Could be smoke," he called down. "Seems to lay low on the water."

Tracy was summoned from his cabin and took a look through the glasses. Then he ordered the stokers below to get up steam and told Anse to change his course two points south. Within twenty minutes the question was settled. Moving along the horizon were three good-sized steamers, headed on a course that would intercept the *Sea Sprite's.*

At that point Hobe Gaskill showed up to relieve Anse. His long face was drawn down in lines of worry, and he shook his head as he took the wheel.

"I told ye things was goin' too good," he growled. "Now we got to dodge a whole fleet o' Yankee cruisers."

Immediately the crew was called to strike sail. The blockade runner's best chance to get through was to remain invisible as long as possible. The good Welsh coal in her bunkers made very little smoke, and with her canvas stowed, her gray coloring blended with the ocean.

The enemy ships were still hull down, six or seven miles distant. Tracy ordered the runner's course changed again, and the bow swung northeastward as the engines chugged at half speed. If this maneuver brought the cruisers about, they would know the *Sea Sprite* had been sighted.

For several minutes the three larger ships continued toward the south. Then the lookout reported the first one in line was making a turn. At once Tracy went hurrying up the rigging to see for himself. Another minute passed while he studied the men-of-war through his powerful glasses. Then he came down. There was a grin of excitement on his handsome face as he strode aft to the wheel.

"Boys," he announced, "we should have some sport out of this! Two of those ships are brig-rigged and look pretty slow. But the third one's newer and has better lines. From what I can see of her, I'd say she's the *Niphon* or a cruiser of her class. You've all heard of the *Niphon*—supposed to be the terror of the blockade. Let's show her what a real runner can do!"

He rang the engine room for full speed ahead and told Hobe to hold the same northeasterly course. Sunset was still more than an hour away, but off to port a gray cloud bank had appeared over the sea. It was toward this cover that they steered, slicing through the swells at a racing clip. The log line showed they were making a full thirteen knots—all the speed possible with their deckload of cotton. Yet when Anse glanced at the cruiser, off to starboard, he was disturbed to see she had gained on them.

A short time later the firing began. The range was still

very long, even for rifled guns. The *Niphon* must have been close to four miles south of them. But they could hear the boom of her cannon plainly and see the white spouts of spray where the shells fell short.

"Mr. Calhoun!" the skipper ordered. "Call all hands to get sail on her. We'll see if we can't add a knot or two."

Anse sprinted aft to the main halyards, where he was joined by old Mike Rudge. The grizzled sailor had served many years in the Navy in the days of sail, and he could handle running rigging with a master's touch. They had the mainsail drawing a full minute before the rest of the crew finished setting the foresail and jibs.

At Tracy's command the *Sea Sprite* had swung due north and was running close-hauled. Her narrow stern silhouette would offer a smaller target to the cruiser's cannoneers. Anse heard the muffled report of another gun and saw the shell fall right abeam—a bare forty yards away.

He had been under fire often enough before but always in the dark of night. This was broad daylight, and the aim was getting uncomfortably close. He knew the fear a rabbit must feel, hopping across an open field with guns banging right behind.

Rudge chuckled and shot a stream of tobacco juice over the lee side. "Ain't one chance in fifty they kin hit us," he remarked. "An' we'll be hid by the fog 'fore they kin git in decent range."

Ahead of the little ship, Anse could see the gray mist thick on the sea. It was still more than a mile off, but the runner was holding her own now. Another cannon shot fell astern. Soon the first wisps of fog swept by, and within minutes the gray shroud had completely surrounded them. The boy drew a long breath of relief.

Hobe Gaskill had changed to a new course when Anse took over the helm. The heading was now a point south of east, and he was told to hold it as long as they had the protection of the fog. Night had begun to fall now, made darker by the mist. The hooded binnacle lamp was the only light allowed aboard the *Sea Sprite*. After dark no man could so much as strike a match. And the rule was rigidly enforced.

The engines were running at half speed to save coal, but with the breeze over the port quarter they still plowed along at eight or nine knots. Anse only hoped they wouldn't meet a fellow blockade runner steaming west in the murky dark. It was nearing midnight, and his trick was almost over when he heard a faint chunking of paddles through the fog. Then a startled exclamation came from the foretop.

"A ship!" the lookout called in a hushed voice. "Cut right across our bows, so close I could ha' tossed a biscuit aboard her!"

"Which way was she headed?" Tracy asked calmly.

"North, sir."

The captain turned back to the wheel. "Hold her as she is, O'Neal," he said. "I've an idea that Yankee skipper was trying to outsmart us. Lucky he didn't run us under, at that."

Shakily Anse gripped the spokes, his eyes on the compass. Once more it seemed as if a special Providence watched over the little *Sea Sprite*. After he had been relieved, he went to his bunk but found it hard to get to sleep. Where, he wondered, would the hunters be when daylight came? At last he dozed off, but it seemed only a moment later when he was roused by the call of "All hands on deck!"

Staggering out into the first gray of daylight, he saw that the fog had begun to lift. Wispy streamers of mist swept past the ship, carried on a brisk morning wind. Before he had time even for a cup of coffee, he was sent aloft to relieve the lookout.

The breeze was from the northwest, and at this hour it was cold enough to make him shiver. He gripped the stays beside his perch, rubbed the sleep out of his eyes, and stared into the scattering fog. The *Sea Sprite* was still under full sail. It was hard to judge her speed with a following sea, but he could tell by the quickened slap of the paddles that MacIvor had a head of steam up.

Within five minutes the fog was gone. Anse could see the horizon now in all directions, and to his deep relief there was no sign of smoke or sail. Somehow they had dodged their pursuers in the night.

When he finally came down and got his breakfast, the sun was well up and the day was fair. Forward by the turtle-back Mike Rudge was splicing a rope, and Anse went to join him.

"Well," the old seaman remarked, "we still got our hides. The skipper o' that fast Yank cruiser wasn't so dumb, though. He figgered we'd change course toward Bermuda once we was in the fog, so he swung over to head us off. If Tracy'd turned east half a minute sooner, we'd ha' been hit squar' amidships."

"Where do you reckon he is now?" Anse asked. "An' what about the other two?"

"The *Niphon* likely kep' on north a spell, an' mebbe we lost her. Them others? Ain't no tellin', but if I was in command o' the squadron, I'd ha' had 'em hold east along the edge o' the fogbank. 'Twon't surprise me none if we sight 'em pretty soon."

Rudge's guess proved to be accurate enough. Just as the captain was taking his noonday reading of the sun, the man in the crow's nest hailed the deck.

"Smoke to starboard, sir," he called. "Two ships, hull down."

Tracy put aside his sextant and went aloft. When he had studied the southern horizon a moment, he returned to Gaskill at the wheel.

"They're Federals, for certain," he said, "but I doubt if they've enough speed to catch us." He whistled the engine room and got MacIvor on the speaking tube.

"How's your coal, Mac?" he asked. "Got enough left for fast steaming?"

Anse couldn't hear the reply, but the engineer must have inquired about the distance still to go.

"We're still two hundred miles from St. George," Tracy told him. "All right, save it all you can, then. The enemy's in sight, about six miles south of us, but they may not have spotted us."

A few minutes later he ordered Anse to take the lookout. "Keep a close watch on that pair," he said. "Let me know at once if they change course or put on more steam. And don't forget to look north every little while. The *Niphon* might show up any time."

The boy followed his instructions to the letter. The double smoke cloud off to starboard gradually fell astern, and it seemed that the *Sea Sprite,* with her almost smokeless coal, had slipped past without being detected. He began to concentrate more on the horizon to port.

The first warning came as a tiny smudge, no bigger than a man's hand. Immediately he hailed the deck, and the captain climbed to a position just below him, bringing his binoculars to bear on the suspicious patch of gray.

"That's our Yankee friend, sure enough," Tracy said with a grin. "I doubt if he's raised us yet, but keep an eye on him."

It was then only about three o'clock in the afternoon. If there was to be a chase, it would be in daylight, and there was no hint of any friendly fog to hide them. Anse settled himself with an arm around the mast and glued his eyes to the smoke smudge. Little by little it grew larger. Then, at the end of an hour or more, he could make out spars and topmasts. The cruiser was steaming on a course roughly parallel to theirs but gradually narrowing the distance.

A few minutes after that Anse was relieved at the foretop and told to take over the helm from Hobe Gaskill. As he steered, he told the captain how things stood.

"Don't seem as if they've sighted us," he said, "but they're movin' a couple o' knots faster'n we are."

Tracy nodded. "That's likely enough," he answered. "The wind's died, and we're only using the engines at a bit more than half speed. Last time we heaved the log we were doing under ten knots."

He went forward once more and up the ratlines, taking a long look at the other ship. When he came down, he ordered the sails lowered. Then he asked MacIvor for more steam. The revolutions of the paddles came at a faster beat, and Anse could feel the runner surge ahead beneath him. Twenty minutes passed, and he heard the sailor on the log line hail the bridge.

"Twelve an' a half!" his sing-song voice announced.

The cruiser's smoke could be seen clearly from the deck now. She seemed to be making about the same speed as the *Sea Sprite,* but her distance abeam was growing narrower. If her lookouts were alert, Anse thought, they must surely have sighted the smaller ship. Soon, he decided, they would be within range for a broadside.

Captain Tracy stayed halfway up the rigging and kept his glasses trained on the enemy. Calhoun was down in the engine room. After a little while he emerged from the hatch and called to the skipper.

"Mac says he's only got coal for about ten more hours if he has to keep the pressure this high," the mate reported.

"Tell him not to worry." Tracy laughed. "We'll burn

cotton if we have to. But ask him first if he has plenty of coal dust handy. I'll tell him when to use it."

Coal dust, Anse knew, was never burned in ordinary circumstances. It threw up a black smoke that could be seen many miles away. He wondered if the captain had some kind of trick up his sleeve.

Another hour passed, and the Yankee cruiser, still off the port beam, was edging nearer. Nervously Anse waited for orders to change course. Then Tracy climbed down and sauntered past the wheel.

"As she is, sir?" Anse asked.

The captain nodded. "Same course," he said. "Time enough to change when they begin firing."

He went on aft and entered his cabin. Anse felt the sweat start to run down his forehead. The breeze had gone completely, and the air felt oppressively heavy. If he had been at home on Pamlico Sound, he'd have headed for harbor. The day felt like a weather breeder.

About five-thirty the young helmsman heard what he had been unconsciously waiting for—the dull boom of a cannon shot. There was a scurrying of bare feet on deck as the crew climbed the bales to stare northward. Tracy came from the cabin at once and aimed his binoculars at the other vessel.

"They're still out of range," Anse heard him tell Calhoun. "We may get some weather to help us soon. Barometer's falling fast."

Again a report came from one of the Federal ship's big guns. This time it must have been a swivel in the bow, for Anse could see the cruiser was headed straight toward them. The shell fell nearly half a mile abeam, throwing up a huge white waterspout.

Still Tracy chatted with the mate, cool and unconcerned. Another shot came and then another, as the Yankee gunners tested the range. It wasn't until a shell

whistled through the main shrouds that the captain bestirred himself. He went to the speaking tube and called
down to MacIvor.

"Start firing up with that dust," he told the engineer.
"Fast, now, and plenty of it! We'll try making our own
fog."

Three

Almost at once a cloud of choking smoke poured from the stacks. It threw a vast black pall over the runner's wake and spread low along the water with no wind to carry it away. Even on the deck the smoke hung thick, and Anse coughed and wiped his eyes. Then the captain was there at his elbow.

"Start bringing your helm over," came the order. "Easy at first. I want a slow turn to port."

Gradually the boy took the little ship around in an arc that had her headed north at the end of two or three minutes.

"Good!" said Tracy. "Hold her that way till I give you the new course."

The cruiser continued firing in spite of having lost her target. Once, at the beginning of the turn, another shell had fallen close aboard, but now the shots were missing by a wide margin. The *Sea Sprite* skirted the eastern edge of the dense, drifting smoke cloud, doubling back past her pursuer. She had made two or three miles to the northward, still protected by the smoke screen, when Tracy ordered another turn, this time to starboard.

In the meantime, the firemen had stopped feeding coal dust to the boilers. The runner soon emerged into clearer air, back on her eastward course. And somewhere far to the south in the thick of the smoke pall, the cruiser charged on, the sounds of her gunfire growing fainter and fainter.

Hobe Gaskill was chuckling when he took over the helm. "You'll never see a slicker job o' work," he told Anse. "The skipper sure outfoxed 'em that time. Now all we got to worry about is makin' port 'fore the storm hits us."

"You think there's one on the way?" asked Anse. "It sure feels like it. How's the glass look now?"

"Down to twenty-nine an' fallin'," the pilot replied. "Don't fergit—it's September. Hurricane time."

The captain must have had the same thing in mind. He took another sight on the setting sun, now almost hidden in the smoke astern. Then he checked the chronometer and did some fast calculating.

"Seventy miles to go," he told Gaskill. "That means we'll have to run the reefs in the dark. The way the weather looks, I wouldn't dare try to wait outside till morning."

Hobe nodded soberly. "We kin make it all right, sir, if we go in slow an' take plenty o' soundin's. Coal must be about finished, though, I reckon."

"Yes," said Tracy. "It may last till nightfall. After that we can burn cotton and turpentine if we have to, and the smoke won't show in the dark."

"Too bad!" Hobe answered, shaking his head. "Cotton at ninety cents a pound, too! But it's better'n goin' to the bottom."

A few minutes later Anse was sent to the crow's nest with orders to watch the sea in all directions. "We might sight the *Niphon* again," the skipper told him. "Or there could be another cruiser hove to off the Chub Heads. Hail me the minute you sight breakers."

Darkness was settling over the ocean, but there was still enough afterglow astern to show no pursuit in that quarter. The boy concentrated on the horizon ahead. When it was fully dark, he caught the pungent odor of turpentine and saw thick smoke coming from the funnels. MacIvor must have run out of coal. Anse wondered how many five-hundred-dollar bales of cotton would have to be sacrificed to get them into St. George.

It was nearly eleven that night when his eyes caught the glimmer of surf on the southeastern horizon.

"Breakers, ho!" he called down. "They're four points off the starboard bow."

"Good enough," Calhoun's voice answered. "I'll tell the cap'n. That must be the North Rocks, from the way we're headed."

Tracy verified the surf with his binoculars and ordered the vessel's course changed somewhat to port. Anse understood the reason, for he knew the long line of wicked reefs that fringed the north coast of the islands. Within another hour or two they had safely weathered the Kitchen Shoals and were swinging down the shore toward Five Fathom Hole. Two leadsmen were in the bows, constantly calling the soundings, while the *Sea Sprite* moved cautiously, her paddles barely turning. Then they were in the narrow channel above St. David's Head and steaming slowly northwestward into the wide reaches of the harbor.

From his perch aloft Anse could see a hundred lights on shore and in the anchorage. Midnight though it was, St. George was far from asleep. Loud voices raised in drunken song came across the water from the taverns, and the figures of stevedores could be seen moving cotton bales on the waterfront. Every berth at the docks appeared to be full.

"All right, lads," Tracy told the crew. "We'll drop anchor here and wait for morning to unload cargo. Once we're at moorings, you can all turn in."

Anse was glad to clamber down. He was more tired than

he had realized, and even the straw pallet in his berth felt good to his weary body. Within five minutes he was sound asleep, in spite of the rising gusts of wind that rocked the ship.

*　　*　　*

The loud creak of cordage and the sudden heeling of the ship brought him awake about two-thirty in the morning. Still drowsy, he thought they must be at sea once more. Then he heard the screaming of the wind, as the ship lay over dizzily to starboard. Rain lashed the side of the forecastle, and streams of water ran in through the companionway. The storm that had been threatening was on them at last.

Anse staggered up and pulled on his boots and oilskins. The galley fire was out, and the cook was still asleep, so there would be no breakfast aboard. Forward, on the slanting deck, he found Hobe Gaskill and the mate anxiously watching the mooring cable. Even though the harbor was sheltered from the full force of the gale, there was danger that the ship would drag her anchor. As more of the crew arrived, they bent another cable to the spare anchor and dropped it from the stern. Then, in the lee of the dripping bales, they huddled and waited for the wind and the deluge to moderate.

Finally, at seven o'clock in the morning, the cook succeeded in starting a fire, and mugs of hot black coffee took some of the chill out of their bones. Beans and hardtack followed. And well before noon the wind had gone down enough to let a boat put off for shore. Anse was among the rowers. They landed at one of the piers, and Tracy hurried off to talk to the *Sea Sprite's* owners.

When he came back, the skies were clearing, and the captain looked more cheerful. Anse hastened to round up the oarsmen who had dropped into the nearest bar.

"Come on, men," Tracy told them. "Snap to it, now. We'll be warping her into a berth in the next hour. When the cargo's ashore, you'll get all the leave you want."

Late that afternoon, when the little blockade runner was alongside her pier, Anse watched the cotton going ashore. The Negro roustabouts who handled it spoke a garbled English dialect that made him chuckle every time he heard it. He counted the bales. Seven hundred and forty of them had come safely through the Federal cordon. He knew the price in Wilmington was ten cents a pound, and here in Bermuda the latest quotation was almost a dollar. Tobacco, turpentine, and pine tar brought equally fantastic profits. It was no wonder that the commission men who bought and sold cotton in St. George drank imported champagne every night and had their carriage horses decked out in silver-mounted harness. Sometimes he saw them and their friends, the blockade-running captains, toss whole bags of English shillings to the little Negroes who followed them about.

Many of the skippers, Anse had heard, received five thousand or more for each round trip. He supposed Captain Tracy got at least that much. But while some of the men who commanded runners added to their gains by carrying only luxury goods on the return voyage, he knew Tracy was different. On every trip Anse had made in the *Sea Sprite,* she had been loaded with arms and supplies for the Confederate fighting men. Cases of Enfield rifles and carbines usually filled part of her hold, along with cartridges, powder and lead, flour and bacon. In his own cabin the captain would stow the precious medicines and surgical implements desperately needed by army doctors. If he added a few cases of brandy, bolts of silk, or bottles of perfume, they were usually intended as gifts for friends at home.

At sunset that evening Anse accompanied Hobe Gaskill

on a visit to the town. Instead of heading for Shinbone Alley or one of the other sailors' haunts, the pair went up a white-paved street leading away from the noisy waterfront. It was an old street, quiet, flanked by stately houses built of coral blocks. To a boy from the Outer Banks, these Bermuda houses had a strange beauty and dignity. Each sat in its own little garden, bright with hibiscus and bougainvillea. Close to each house was a buttery, also of stone blocks and with a pyramid-shaped roof. Some of the residences were white, others tinted in soft pink or green or blue. Near the crest of the hill, Hobe stopped in front of a long flight of steps leading up to a very old church.

"That there's St. Peter's," he told Anse. "They tell me she was built more'n two hundred an' fifty years back—1612, if I ain't mistook. Purty, ain't she?"

There was still some light in the sky, and they found their way back to the ancient graveyard, close to the square church tower. Among the cedars were tombstones so old that the names carved on them had all but worn away, and some of the stones themselves had fallen and crumbled.

"Folks been here a long time," said Hobe solemnly. "But they got a nice, friendly place to lie in."

When they returned to the busier part of town, they tried to find rooms at one of the two hotels. Both men had plenty of money, but it did them very little good. There wasn't a bed to be had.

"Oh, well," said Anse, "I'd just as soon sleep aboard. Now the cotton's gone, there's room to stretch out on deck, an' it looks like a fine, clear night."

They brought blankets from their bunks and spread them aft of the paddle boxes. For a little while Anse was content to lie there looking up at the bright stars. Then, oblivious to the shouting and laughter from the waterfront a stone's throw away, he drifted off to sleep.

*　　*　　*

When morning came, there was a lot of activity in the harbor. Two or three blockade runners, stormbound in St. George during the gale, were getting ready to go out. There was a theory along the docks that any Federal cruisers lurking outside must have been blown off their stations by the storm, and this would be a safe time to start.

Mike Rudge watched their preparations for departure with a jaundiced eye. "Durn' fools!" he growled. "The Navy don't git chased off by a little blow like that. Why, when I was in the ol' *Constellation,* we rid out hurricanes twicet as bad an' never lost our bearin's."

He spat over the side and staggered off to his bunk. Anse knew most of the old tar's temper this morning was caused by a rough night in the taverns.

The long, slim steamers finished their coaling and chugged out through the channel, the Confederate flags flying gaily from their main trucks. Shortly after they had gone, a big British packet came up the narrows and moved majestically to her moorings. She dwarfed most of the vessels at the docks and at anchor. Soon Anse saw a boat lowered from her side, and several gentlemen in top hats were rowed ashore.

Under Calhoun's orders all the crew who were sober enough had been holystoning the *Sea Sprite's* decks that morning. The standing rigging, torn by the *Niphon's* fire, had already been repaired. As soon as her return cargo was loaded and her bunkers filled with Cardiff coal, the runner could put to sea. Through the rest of the day, however, nothing happened.

About sunset Captain Tracy, who had spent the night at a hotel, came down to the dock. His clothes were spick-and-span, and his step was as jaunty as ever. As soon as he came aboard, he called the mate, the engineer, and the pilot to his cabin. Their conference there lasted nearly two hours, and when they came out, they were smiling broadly.

Anse learned the reason from Hobe Gaskill later that evening.

"There's a bran'-new ship in port," Hobe told him, glancing around to make sure they weren't overheard. "You can't see her from here, but she's tucked away in the furtherest berth, over yonder. The skipper's been talkin' to the agents all afternoon, an' they've offered her to him if he wants her."

"You mean she's better'n the *Sprite?*" Anse asked in unbelief.

"No tellin' till we've looked her over. But she's got the latest thing in engines, an' her b'ilers are built with tubes —to give her higher steam pressure. More'n that, she's got no paddles—jest screws. One shaft on each engine! The builders claim she'll do better'n fifteen knots loaded, but o' course MacIvor won't believe it."

"Whew!" Anse breathed. "Boy! You reckon we could get a peek at her?"

"I dunno. But I'm invited to go see her tomorrer. Mebbe the cap'n won't mind if you tag along. Mind, now —don't say a word about this. Plenty of other skippers'd give their eye teeth to sail her."

"Don't you worry, Hobe," Anse replied. "I'll keep my mouth tight shut. Only tell me—what's her name?"

"The *Gray Witch,*" Gaskill whispered.

Four

The packet had brought mail and newspapers from London, and next morning the waterfront was crowded with commission men, speculators, and runner captains, discussing the news. Most of them were British and Bermudians, with quite a scattering of Confederate agents. The sympathies of the port were almost solidly for the South. Anse, idling on the deck, saw only one Northerner —the United States consul. He was a glum-looking gentleman from Boston, who stalked along the street without speaking to anyone. His sharp eyes, however, were constantly glancing at the various blockade runners and sizing up their state of readiness.

Hobe came along after a few minutes. "How 'bout takin' a little walk up that-a-way," he suggested with a wink. And Anse quickly agreed.

They strolled along the waterfront, stopping occasionally before the big warehouses—W. L. Penno's, J. W. Musson's, and John Tory Bourne's. Bourne was one of the wealthiest men in the islands and acted as commercial agent for the Confederate Government. His huge estate, Rose Hill, was the show place of St. George. It was there that Ransome Tracy and other captains were frequently entertained.

"Heard some pretty good news in the tavern last night," said Gaskill. "A couple o' mates from the packet were there, an' accordin' to their tell, the war'll be over 'fore Christmas."

"You mean England's goin' to recognize the Confederate States an' come in on our side?" Anse asked eagerly.

"No. Ain't much chance o' that right now. But the bettin's all on McClellan bein' elected president, an when that happens, the Democrats'll want to stop fightin'. These Britishers, they figger it won't even last till McClellan takes office."

"Gee!" said Anse. "You reckon we can get in a couple o' more runs before that?"

Gaskill laughed. "Sounds like you really like this business," he replied. "Me, I don't 'specially hanker to git shot at or stuck in a Yankee prison. Still, it's a good livin', long as we stay lucky."

"If the skipper gets this new ship," Anse explained, "I'd sort o' like to see how she handles, is all. That must be her, over yonder."

They soon found they were not the only ones with an interest in the new blockade runner. A dozen officers and seamen from other ships were admiring, criticizing, and arguing about her when they approached. A truculent, red-faced mate off the *Sweet Annie* was the loudest of the group.

"I never had no use fer a steel hull," he announced. "Them thin three-sixteenth-inch plates'll buckle an' start the first time you try to run through any kind of a storm. An' if they're made any heavier, it slows you down. No, sir—give me live oak an' cedar every time!"

"This 'un's got half-inch plates, so they say," a milder voice answered. "She's sure 'nough got pretty lines, anyhow. Looks fast to me."

The critical mate snorted. "Not to me!" he said. "I call her ugly. No paddle boxes. That straight deck line makes her look durn' near naked!"

Grinning, Hobe took Anse's arm and drew him away. "Leave 'em rave," he said. "We'll git a better look this afternoon when we go aboard her. I'm hungry now. What say we find us a place to eat?"

There was a small dining room a few doors down the street, and there they reveled in roast chicken and vegetables, English muffins and jam—things the galley of the *Sea Sprite* never had.

"Always was partial to chicken," Hobe remarked when the coffee came. "I heard a yarn about chickens aboard a runner. This was a couple o' years back—on the ol' *Palmetto,* if I ain't mistook. Her skipper liked to eat good, so he had the cook take along a coop o' live hens an' roosters. Seems there was jest one young rooster left when they got south o' Cape Lookout on the trip home.

"That was before the blockade got so tight, but cruisers hung around there jest the same. It was a fine dark night —no moon an' the tide was settin' right. The *Palmetto* had every light doused, tarps over the paddle boxes to deaden the sound, an' all the crew was barefoot or wearin' rope sandals fer quiet.

"Along about three in the mornin' they'd steamed to within five miles o' the bar. All of a sudden they spotted a Yank gunboat layin' right ahead, not more'n a cable's length off. The skipper had the engines cut way down so they could sneak past. They were doin' fine, movin' silent as a ghost, an' they'd jest laid the gunboat astern when that durn' rooster started to crow!"

Anse was listening, openmouthed. "What happened?" he asked.

"Oh, nothin' much. They'd put on full speed an' pulled half a mile away 'fore the gunboat could start firin'. One lucky shot hit the afterdeck an' knocked the chicken coop overboard. You might say it served the rooster right, but he was dead already. The cook had wrung his neck. I reckon that's the last live chicken that ever traveled through the blockade."

In the street outside, the sun blazed down, and the activity of the waterfront had slackened, as it usually did during the heat of the day. Hobe and Anse made their way back to the *Sea Sprite* and napped a while in the shade of a deck awning. Shortly after three they were roused by the mate.

"Cap'n Tracy's ready to go ashore," he told Gaskill. "Come on an' stir yourself."

The pilot rose and put on his shoes and his white duck uniform jacket. A moment later the captain appeared with MacIvor.

"Sir," said Hobe, "could I ask a favor? I'd sort o' like to take young O'Neal along if you're willin'."

Calhoun scowled, but Tracy was affable enough. "I don't see why not," he replied. "He's a good lad at the helm and knows enough to keep his mouth shut."

They sauntered up the waterfront, Anse keeping well to the rear. There were few people on the street. It would be another hour before most of the town came out to start carousing in the cool of the evening. About the time the four reached the *Gray Witch's* dock, a carriage drawn by a smart pair of matched black horses pulled up beside them. A Negro footman jumped down and opened the door with a flourish. And out stepped a large, florid gentleman in a top hat.

Tracy went forward, smiling. "Mr. Bourne," he said, "how do you do today?"

"Tolerably well, thank you, Captain," said Bourne, "considering all the Madeira I drank last night. Shall we go aboard?"

There were introductions when they reached the deck. "Mr. MacIvor and Mr. Calhoun I believe you've met, sir," said Tracy. "This is Mr. Gaskill, our pilot, and Mr. O'Neal, who acts as assistant pilot."

Anse flushed at the new title and bowed stiffly to the famous agent. Then he followed the others down to the engine room.

"The hull," Bourne was explaining, "was built in Liverpool. The boilers and the engines, though, were shipped down from the Clyde. What do you think of 'em, MacIvor?"

The old Scotsman didn't commit himself at once. He peered cautiously into the nearest boiler, feeling the steel tubes with his gnarled hands. Then he opened a firebox door and clanged it shut. Last, he knelt beside one of the beautifully machined engines, examining its novel features.

"Aye," he said at length. "Nae doot she'll run."

Bourne and Tracy roared with laughter. "That's high praise from Mac," said the captain. "But he won't be sure till he's made a trip or two. What's the top pressure these boilers'll take?"

"On the voyage out from the Mersey," Bourne replied, "they had steam up to forty pounds several times. And the British crew that brought her swears they were logging eighteen knots."

Tracy whistled. "For a ship that's barely broken in," he said, "she sounds like a real racer. I take it she's a bit bigger than the *Sprite?*"

"Two hundred and twenty feet overall," Bourne answered with a nod. "Twenty-one-foot beam. Draws eight feet loaded. You can't beat those dimensions for a runner, can you? And look at the bunkers. They'll hold coal enough to take you nearly two thousand miles."

From the engine room they went above deck to inspect the crew's quarters and cabins for the officers. Here the new ship showed a marked improvement over the *Sea*

Sprite. The forecastle was lighter and more spacious. And there were five good-sized compartments aft. The captain's cabin itself seemed as big as a ballroom to Anse. It had two comfortable-looking berths, a desk and chart box, and a handsome teakwood table large enough to seat six people.

"Ah," said Tracy with a chuckle, "now I'm beginning to be interested. A captain who wanted to make his fortune could stow a lot of luxury goods in here. Not that I'm inclined that way, but at least there's room to stretch out in comfort and to entertain a few guests."

He turned to Calhoun and Gaskill. "What do you think of her, boys?" he asked.

"Can't say till I see how she'd stand up to a storm," the mate replied. "I've heard o' some steel ships where the plates buckled. The old *Banshee* was one."

Bourne smiled. "I think I can reassure you on that point," said he. "This ship ran through a gale, crossing the Bay of Biscay, and as you can see, the plates took no damage."

"There's a couple o' things I like about her," Hobe put in. "She ought to run quieter'n the *Sprite,* with no paddles to slap the waves. An' if I ain't mistook, her exhaust comes out under water. That'd be a help if we had to stop the engines in the middle of a mess o' Yanks. Remember how we've near got caught blowin' off steam?"

Tracy nodded thoughtfully. "I'd like to wait a day or two," he told Bourne, "before I give you an answer. The *Sea Sprite's* old, but she's served us well. We know her and trust her."

"Very well, Captain," the agent agreed. "Take your time to think it over. Not too long, though. General Lee needs the cargo we've got waiting."

They went down the gangplank to the dock, and John

Tory Bourne got into his carriage. The others walked back to their ship.

"Well, youngster," Tracy said to Anse, "what did you think of her? We haven't heard from you."

"She's mighty pretty, sir," the boy replied. "I'd want to see how she answers her helm, o' course, but from just lookin' at her, I'd like to sail in her."

"There's one thing none of you mentioned," said the captain. "Did you notice her smokestacks? They're built to fold down almost to the deck. That's a new wrinkle—supposed to make her harder to see. I'm not so sure I like it, though."

"Nor I," MacIvor chimed in. "They'd hae to be up to gie her any draft."

At the *Sea Sprite* they separated, Tracy going up to his hotel, the mate and the engineer to one of the waterside taverns. Anse and the pilot sat under a deck awning till suppertime.

It was nearing sunset when a blockade runner came limping into St. George harbor. Her foremast and one funnel had been shot away, and the starboard paddle box was in splinters. More important, she appeared to be down by the head.

"Hey!" said Anse. "Isn't that one o' the ships that went out right after the storm?"

" 'Tis so," his friend agreed. "The *Razee*, sure's a gun's iron! She's sinkin', too. Look—they're goin' to beach her."

Wallowing on past the anchorage and the docks, the damaged runner barely succeeded in making shore. Her bow grated on the coral, and she settled in the water, heeling over toward the town. At once boats put off to her from nearby piers. They took off her crew and unloaded as much of the cargo as possible before her stern went under.

At supper in their favorite public house, Anse and

Hobe heard the story of what had happened. The three blockade runners had left the harbor together in broad daylight, then separated, each choosing a different course. The *Razee* had taken the southern route, sailing down past Tucker's Town and keeping well out to avoid the rocks. By sunset the ship had left the Gibbs Hill light-house far astern and was heading for the open ocean.

Just before dark, the lookout had sighted smoke to the northward. They changed course a little to keep away, though at that time the captain thought it was probably one of the other runners. As soon as night fell, the *Razee* steamed on, her crew confident that they were safe.

But with the first morning light a large ship was seen only four miles away and right in their path. Hastily, the runner came about. Sure that they had been sighted, the skipper headed back for Bermuda. They had a favoring breeze from the west and plenty of coal, so they fled at top speed. One of the crew was willing to swear that while he was heaving the log, they were making better than fifteen knots.

Unhappily, as they soon discovered, they were being chased by one of the fastest cruisers in the U.S. Navy—the *Rhode Island*. Little by little the ship gained on them, and before noon shells were beginning to fall uncomfortably close. Frantically, the *Razee* clawed on eastward. She was within sight of the coastline, about eight miles from Southampton, when the cruiser got within range. A shell exploded close over the bow, smashing the foremast and throwing the lookout to the deck with a broken leg. Soon another shell demolished the forward stack and one of the paddle boxes, and a round shot went through the foredeck and the hold, putting a big hole in the bottom.

By luck the engines were still functioning well. Before the cruiser could sink her quarry, they were inside the three-mile limit, in British territorial waters. There was nothing for the *Rhode Island* to do but veer off and give up the chase. The crew of the runner manned the pumps and succeeded in keeping her afloat just long enough to reach St. George.

There was little sympathy for the vessel's misfortune among the seamen ashore. As Hobe put it, her officers had brought it on themselves by leaving in daylight. The cruiser must have sighted them before nightfall and figured out where they would be at dawn.

"Anyhow," the pilot added, "they were lucky to have only one man hurt. An' they saved most o' the cargo. That's a heap better'n bein' in Davy Jones's locker."

Five

News was buzzing along the waterfront when Anse and Hobe went ashore next morning.

"You chaps are luckier'n you know," a young British sailor told Anse. "All the scuttlebutt is that you're takin' the *Gray Witch* out. Me an' my mates come over in her, an' she's a sweetheart, no fear."

"Why do ye think we'd want her?" Hobe laughed at him. "Nothin' wrong with the runner we got."

Nevertheless, the rumors persisted. At noon Captain Tracy came aboard the *Sea Sprite* and had the men mustered aft.

"You may have heard some talk," he said. "Well, it's true. Now that the *Razee's* lost, her owners need a new ship, and it's been decided they'll buy this one. We're transferring to the *Gray Witch*. Get your duffel out and put it in her fo'c'sle. You all know where she lies.

"Now," he went on, "we'll be loading cargo tonight and tomorrow. I want every man to stay reasonably sober because we'll be sailing tomorrow night. Any one of you who doesn't report in good condition will find himself on the beach."

With that he dismissed them and went ashore for more consultations with Bourne. Anse hurried to gather his belongings and carry his sea bag up to the new ship. He was among the first to reach her forecastle and secured one of the best berths, close to the entrance.

Almost at once drays from the warehouses began to roll up to the *Gray Witch's* gangplank. Her hatches were opened, and the dock hands lowered boxes and barrels into the hold. There were huge, heavy cases from England marked "hardware," which Anse was pretty sure contained repeating Enfield carbines for the Confederate cavalry. Many of the kegs, too, looked suspiciously like gunpowder. These were stowed well forward, away from the boilers and the engine room.

All the while the cargo was being taken on, Calhoun examined the rigging and sails, and MacIvor stayed below, studying the engines. Hobe and Anse went to the pilothouse. Instead of being on the open deck, as in the *Sea Sprite,* the wheel and binnacle were raised three or four feet and housed in a glassed-in enclosure with a roof over it.

"This oughta help some in bad weather," the pilot commented. "Won't have to stand waist-deep in every sea that comes aboard."

In midafternoon Anse, who had been wanting to swim in the warm Bermuda water, stripped down to a pair of short drawers and slipped over the side. The water wasn't as clear here by the docks as off the beaches, but it was still inviting. For a while he was content to paddle around the ship on the surface. Then he dove under her counter and swam downward, holding onto the rudder. He wanted a look at the twin screws, new in his experience.

There they were, one on each side of the tapering stern. Through the translucent water their heavy bronze blades gleamed, and when he touched the metal, it felt as smooth as velvet. As long as he had breath, he stayed there examining the carefully sealed bearings, where the shafts came out of the hull. Leakage around a propeller shaft, he had heard, was a possible drawback in a screw-driven vessel. But these appeared to be completely watertight.

When he came up, gasping for air, Hobe was leaning over the taffrail. "Reckoned mebbe you was drowned," the pilot remarked. "How's she look under there?"

"Seems to be all shipshape," Anse panted. "Rudder's good an' big, so she ought to steer all right. An' those screws look like they could send her along."

"Fine." Gaskill chuckled. "First time one of 'em fouls a cable, we'll send you down to cut her loose."

Before dark most of the regular cargo had come aboard. In addition to the arms and ammunition, there were cases of shoes, bales of leather, and several tons of staple foods—bacon, flour, and coffee—all hard to get in the South.

Some of the crew had bought luxury items to sell in Wilmington. It was possible, Anse knew, to make a tremendous profit on small things easy to stow under a bunk. Old Mike Rudge, for instance, had purchased several bottles of French perfume. They cost him perhaps twenty dollars in gold, and he boasted he could get forty times that from a fellow he knew in North Carolina. Somehow Anse couldn't bring himself to take part in such dealings. Every time he was tempted, he thought of Lee's soldiers, ragged, hungry, and brave, and knew the trade in luxuries was a dirty business.

One thing he wanted to do, however, was buy presents for his family at home. That evening he persuaded Hobe to go with him to a shop on the waterfront where there were bolts of cloth on display.

"I know my ma hasn't had a new dress in years," he told his friend. "What do you reckon she'd like to wear to church?"

Hobe pointed to a length of gray merino. "That'd be purty," he said. "Warm enough fer winter, too."

Anse agreed and bought enough for a dress. Then he moved on to the cotton goods.

"Here's a nice item," said the storekeeper. "Just in from

Halifax. O' course," he added with a wink, "it was likely
loomed in Boston, but I'll guarantee the cotton came from
the South."

He was pointing at a sprigged muslin that looked light
and attractive. Anse thought of his two small sisters and
got several yards of the material. Finally he bought calico
for everyday dresses and petticoats. His total purchase
came to two pounds, ten shillings.

"That's 'round thirteen dollars, gold," Hobe told him.
"You couldn't buy the cloth fer less'n three hundred in
Wilmington, even if they had it to sell. Reckon your
ma'll be right pleased."

The pilot bought a few trinkets for his sister at home,
then invested in half a dozen pairs of silk stockings as a
speculation. "Some o' them purty gals in Richmond'll be
wearin' these," he told Anse. "So you might say I'm doin'
it in a good cause, even if I do make money out of it."

The next morning Sandy MacIvor got steam up in the
boilers, and they moved the *Gray Witch* over to the coaling docks. There wasn't much coal on hand, but they got
what they hoped would be enough for the voyage. Three
additional stokers had been hired—all Bermuda Negroes.
And at Tracy's insistence, an engineer's helper was signed
on. He was a young man from Glasgow who talked with
even more of a brogue than MacIvor. His name was
Donald Burns.

The new moon was a tiny crescent in the western sky
when the runner was ready for sea that night. They waited
till it had set, then steamed out through the three-fathom
channel of the Town Cut. Outside, the ocean was in
pitchy darkness, but they could feel the long swells rolling
under them. Once they were well clear of the reefs, Gaskill
gave the wheel to Anse.

"She steers like a lady," he said. "You ain't likely to
have any trouble. Just hold her on this course."

When they set the sails, the crew discovered another innovation. All the canvas had been dyed a soft gray-blue in color, and even from the deck it was practically invisible in the dark. With the wind abeam and a good head of steam in the boilers, the *Gray Witch* logged a steady fifteen knots all through Anse's trick at the helm. A little before midnight there was a muffled hail from the foretop.

"Deck ahoy!" came Mike Rudge's croaking voice. "A steamer—half a mile off on the sta'board bow. I smelled her smoke, an' now I kin see her sails."

Tracy was out of his cabin in a jiffy. "Starboard your helm two points," he told Anse as he hurried past the wheelhouse. Swinging the wheel to starboard, of course, meant a turn of the bow to port, away from the other ship. As the boy obeyed, he saw the skipper scrambling up the rigging, night glasses in hand.

"She's a Yankee cruiser," Tracy called down to the mate. "Likely the *Rhode Island*. But she hasn't spotted us yet. You, O'Neal, come back to the original course—due west."

Hobe Gaskill took over the steering at twelve o'clock, and Anse went forward to catch a little sleep. He was called again at two and sent to the crow's nest, relieving Rudge.

"Nothin' stirrin' out there now," the old seaman told him. "Cruiser might ha' been hove to, but she sure had steam up. That soft coal smoke was comin' right downwind to us."

In spite of this reassurance, Anse kept his eyes moving around the dark horizon. If there was one disgrace to a lookout aboard a runner, it was to have a strange sail sighted from the deck before he saw it. In some ships a reward of a dollar was paid the lookout for reporting another craft. But if a man on the deck made the call first, the sailor aloft was docked five dollars.

Two hours passed, and Anse was getting sleepy. Then, just before the time for his relief, he thought he saw a dark shape looming in the distance to the east. Quickly he rubbed his eyes and stared to make sure. Though there was no moon, the night was clear enough to show the line where sea and sky met. And there in the gloom he made out a small dark spot.

"Ahoy, deck!" he hailed. "There's a ship dead astern— 'round five miles off."

Calhoun came up and verified the sighting. He didn't call the captain but whistled the engine room for more steam. The *Gray Witch* answered like a thoroughbred. When the log was heaved a few minutes later, she was speeding westward at a breath-taking eighteen knots. And by daybreak she had left the other ship well below the horizon.

That first day out proved uneventful. They had passed the outer fringe of cruising blockaders and weren't likely to encounter the second cordon—the Gulf Stream fleet— before they were a hundred miles off the coast. In order to avoid reaching that area in daylight, Tracy kept the runner under sail with the engines at little more than idling speed. In the first twenty-four hours at sea, they had logged a total of only two hundred and seventy miles, with some four hundred still to go.

With darkness the stokers began pouring on coal, and they picked up speed again. It was important to be close enough for their final run under the cover of the third night. The lights of a big merchantman showed up about two o'clock in the morning, but the *Gray Witch* slipped past her like a shadow, unobserved. When dawn came, there were two ships on the southern horizon. One, from her low lines and schooner rig, was undoubtedly an outbound Confederate runner. The other, bigger and carrying topsails, looked like a cruiser in pursuit. They were miles apart, and since the little gray steamer seemed to be pulling away handily, there was no point in trying to lure the Yankee off the trail.

Captain Tracy was with Anse in the pilothouse while the young helmsman stood his trick at the wheel.

"How does she answer?" the skipper asked. "Let me take it for a bit."

He swung the spokes two or three points to port and watched the bow come over in a smooth turn. Then he brought her back on course.

"Hm," he said. "Couldn't ask for more. I've an idea we're going to like this craft."

MacIvor came up soon after and added his approval. "A pair o' sweet-runnin' engines, they are," he said, rubbing his hands. "And the young lad ye took on to help me knows his business. Nae doot ye'll be wantin' top speed the nicht, an' we'll gie it to ye."

An hour before sunset, the captain calculated their position as due east of Cape Fear and about a hundred and ten miles out. The crescent moon had grown larger now and set a little later, but they could count on complete darkness by ten o'clock that night.

While there was still some afterglow in the sky, Anse was sent the length of the ship to check on special precautions. Every light was extinguished, and no smoking was allowed. Covers were pulled tightly over the forecastle and cabin ports. Finally he took care of adjusting the tarpaulins over the boiler-room hatch to make sure no glow could be seen when the fire doors were opened. It was tough on the stokers, who worked in 120-degree heat, but they knew it had to be done.

The *Gray Witch* was making about fifteen knots now as she steamed into the dark ahead. The propellers made no noise, and the cutwater was too sharp to throw much of a bow wave. She moved almost as silently as the dim stars overhead.

The breeze was off the land. Tracy had the sails hauled down and stowed, since they could be of little help dead to windward. A little after ten, Anse was sent aloft to take the lookout. He had, the captain seemed to think, the sharpest eyes on the ship, and this would be the most crucial watch of the voyage.

Hardly had the boy settled himself in the crosstrees when his nostrils caught a faint, acrid whiff of soft coal smoke. It was coming downwind from somewhere right ahead. But strain his eyes as he would, he could see nothing resembling a ship. Finally, when the scent came stronger, he hailed the deck. It was Tracy who answered. On this final night the captain would get no sleep.

"I'll come up," he said. "Maybe I can spot her with the night glasses."

Hanging to the rigging just below Anse, he focused his binoculars and peered into the dark where the horizon should be.

"It's pretty hazy," he told the young lookout. "Could be we're running into fog. But you're right about the smoke. I smell it, too."

The runner plowed on without reducing speed. Five minutes passed, then ten. And suddenly, out of the night, two big cruisers appeared. They were only a few hundred yards apart, one to port, the other to starboard. Tracy whistled under his breath and scurried down the ratlines. A few seconds later he was with Gaskill at the wheel. Anse waited, his nerves tense. Surely, he thought, they would veer off or stop the engines, but still the little ship sped on, heading right between the blockaders.

The youngster clung to the mast, hardly daring to breathe. At any instant, he thought, the shells would come crashing aboard. Nearer and nearer loomed the tall hulls. They didn't seem to be moving, but they had steam up. Smoke was drifting from their funnels.

The *Gray Witch* raced almost under the counter of the ship to starboard, and it was only as she shot past that she was seen by the enemy.

"Black snake! Black snake!" came a frenzied cry from the Yankee's stern. It was the call that the blockading fleet used when they sighted a runner.

Six

From Anse's perch, high on the swaying mast, there was an instant when he could look down on the shadowy deck of the cruiser. Lanterns were being lit hastily, and he could hear the pound of running feet as the gunners and powder boys raced to their places. A confused babble of commands rattled out from the ship's officers. All this happened in less than a minute, for the speeding runner was soon a quarter of a mile away. Anse shifted to a more comfortable position and breathed a sigh of relief. He was sure they had now become lost in the darkness.

His feeling of security didn't last long. Suddenly a train of fiery sparks shot up from the cruiser astern, and a rocket burst almost overhead. It was a Drummond light! The great white glare of it hung there in the sky, throwing the two blockade ships into sharp outline and illuminating every inch of the *Gray Witch.*

Half-blinded by the light, Anse cowered closer to the mast. He felt naked and exposed. It was the first time he had seen Drummond lights used, and he had no idea how long the brightness would last. He saw that both cruisers were moving now, ports open and guns run out. It seemed incredible that they had not already started firing.

Then the boom of a cannon came, and a shell whistled close overhead. And at that moment the white flare fizzled out, leaving the darkness even blacker than before. Under

him Anse felt the ship swerve hard to port as the helm was thrown over. A second gun was fired, and then came half a dozen reports together as the cruiser let go her whole broadside. The roar was almost deafening, but the shots flew wild, plowing into the sea where the runner had been a moment before.

Still the *Gray Witch* raced on. Anse could hear the quick scrape of shovels in the hold below and knew the firemen were working like black furies to keep the steam pressure up. It was a lucky thing that the little ship had so much speed, for now the enemy sent up two more rocket lights. In their glare Anse could see the cruisers turning to give chase, but already they had been left a long way astern. He doubted if the dark runner was even visible to their lookouts.

This seemed to be the case, for the firing stopped except for an occasional wild shot from a swivel gun. And the reports sounded farther and farther away.

Shortly, another sailor came up the rigging to take Anse's place. "Skipper wants you at the wheel," he said. The young Ocracoker let himself down to the deck and went at once to the pilothouse. Tracy was humming a little tune under his breath, and his face, in the faint glow from the hooded binnacle, looked cheerful and carefree.

"Those British lads weren't pulling our leg," he was saying to Hobe Gaskill. "She's got all the speed they said she had, and more. Any skipper'd be happy to get nineteen knots when he's in a tight spot."

Hobe relinquished the wheel to Anse with a grin. "We figgered you might like to feel somethin' solid under you fer a change," he said. "When that flare went off, your face looked like a sheet o' white paper up aloft there."

"I don't doubt it," Anse replied sheepishly. "Sure scared the daylights out o' me."

"Jest hold her as she is," the pilot told him. "East, a point north. I'm goin' aft fer a mug-up."

Tracy, too, had left, and Anse was alone with the wheel. He stared ahead into the darkness and hoped the new lookout was alert. If they were through the second line of blockaders, they should have two or three hours of comparative safety. The worst of the run was still to come. But he knew Hobe would be back at the helm when they approached the inner cordon.

*　*　*

It was two-thirty in the morning when Gaskill came to relieve Anse. The pilot shook himself and shivered a little.

"Air feels raw," he said. "There's fog ahead if I know anything about weather. We're in pretty close to the Yankee line, too."

After a moment he sent the boy to fetch the captain. "You reckon we should cut down speed, sir?" he asked when Tracy arrived. "It's gettin' a mite thick."

The skipper looked into the murk and nodded. He called down to MacIvor and ordered half speed on the engines.

In spite of the damp darkness around the ship, Anse had a clear mental picture of the blockading fleet. There would be twenty-five or thirty Yankee gunboats in a ten-mile crescent around Frying Pan Shoals. One end of the line would be close to the surf below Fort Caswell. The other end would hug the shore north of Fort Fisher, keeping just out of range of the big guns.

In one way fog would be a help to the *Gray Witch*. With luck they might slip through without even being seen. But thick weather brought other risks, as Anse well knew. He had heard tales of runners like the *Lola,* which had had the bad fortune to ram her bow squarely into an ironclad gunboat in the fog. Before she could reverse and pull clear, an armed Yankee boarding party was on her deck and she was captured with all hands. That had been more than a year earlier, and the blockade was even tighter now.

There were still three hours till daylight, and by dead reckoning Anse judged they couldn't be much more than twenty miles offshore. Silently the long, low runner steamed through the dark, logging eight or nine knots. No bells rang the hour aboard her, and nobody spoke above a whisper. In the fog, sounds had a way of carrying farther than in clear air.

It was that fact that may have saved their lives half an hour later. Anse was standing at the rail near the pilothouse, straining his eyes into the gloom ahead. He had an uneasy feeling that there was something big and solid out there in the heaving water just beyond his vision. Then he heard a low voice that seemed only fifty feet away, to port.

"Keep an eye peeled," it said. "This is the sort o' night they like."

Tracy, standing with Hobe at the wheel, must have heard it too. But before he could act, one of the Bermuda stokers came stumbling up from the hold for a breath of air. The moment he stepped out into the fog, the man sneezed!

"Hey!" yelled a voice from the gunboat. "Who's there?"

The captain of the *Gray Witch* didn't waste a second. "Look alive!" he yelled back. "Something's moving right astern of you! Black snake! Black snake!"

There was an uproar on the unseen blockader. They could hear running feet, curses, and conflicting commands. And in the confusion Tracy quietly called for full steam ahead. Half a minute later, as the runner sped away, a flare was sent up and several guns boomed. The only effect of the flare was to create a glowing blur in the fog, and the guns were aimed in the wrong direction.

Hobe Gaskill chuckled. "You shore stirred 'em up, sir," he said. "Reckon they're shootin' at each other by now."

"We're not in yet," Tracy warned him. "But I admit it was fun while it lasted. I always wanted to try that trick and never had a chance till now."

A few minutes passed and the captain spoke to Anse. "Go up forward, boy," he said. "Right up on the turtleback. We're turning north now, and I want you to report the first sign of surf."

At the same time leadsmen were dispatched to the fore chains, and speed was reduced once more. Each time the lead was swung, the soundings were a little shallower.

"Mark four!" one seaman called. And then the other, "Quarter less four!"

When the depth was down to three fathoms, Anse thought he heard a distant rumble of breakers. Before he could report it, another sound came to his ears. It was the unmistakable slap of paddle wheels, somewhere off to the right. He scrambled down from the turtleback and raced aft to the wheelhouse.

"Surf to port," he panted. "An' I heard a gunboat to starboard."

Tracy took the news calmly. "Bring her over to port," he told Gaskill. "We'll take a chance on the shoal water."

The wind had begun to freshen a little, and with it the fog started to disperse. The first gray of dawn was beginning to light the sea behind them. Through the remnants of mist, Anse saw the shape of a Federal gunboat a quarter of a mile away. It was sighted by the lookout at the same instant.

"Steady on your course," the captain ordered. "We draw less water than she does."

He whistled down the tube to the engine room and called for more steam. Ahead of them a dim, pale line of surf could now be seen and a low dune behind it.

"Mark twain!" called the leadsman.

"It's all right, sir," Hobe told the captain. "Got my bearin's now. We're four miles north o' the Mound battery. But I'd better bring her over pretty quick 'fore we hit the beach."

"Right you are," said Tracy. "Starboard your helm."

The sharp bow swung over to port as the vessel heeled. And suddenly, without warning, the gunboat started firing. Two shots missed the runner, one falling on each side as she dashed southward. Then, with the boom of the third report, a round shot smashed through the top of the forward stack and hit the pilothouse.

For a moment Anse was stunned. He had been standing only ten feet away, and the jarring crash knocked him to the deck. Then he heard Tracy's sharp command.

"O'Neal! Give us a hand here. Gaskill's been hurt."

Anse scrambled to his feet and reached the raised platform where his friend lay in a pool of blood. A wicked-looking splinter from the wooden canopy protruded from his chest.

"Take the helm," said the captain. "I'll get him aft."

Shaken, the boy gripped the spokes and held the leaping vessel on course. The roar of the surf seemed very close. There was a strong temptation to ease the wheel over a little, but he resisted. The one chance for the *Gray Witch* was to stay in water too shallow for the Yankee to follow. So, paying little attention to the continued firing, he concentrated on his task.

Only two or three minutes could have passed since he took the wheel, but already the sky was lighter. Off to starboard now he could distinguish the grim outline of Fort Fisher's gun emplacements. From them, suddenly, he saw a puff of white smoke blossom out, as one of the big rifled guns thundered a warning to the blockading fleet. And almost at once the gunboat that had been chasing the *Gray Witch* sheered off.

Captain Tracy reappeared at Anse's side. There was still a look of strain on his handsome face, but he gave the boy a smile.

"You've done well, lad," he said. "Had to shave it pretty close, but it's over now. Can you find the New Inlet channel?"

"Yes sir, I think so. What about Hobe, sir? Is he goin' to be all right?"

"He's bleeding a lot," Tracy answered, "but we've got most of it stopped. I think he'll pull through if we can get him to a doctor."

Anse felt better. He could see a break in the line of surf on the bar a few hundred yards ahead. The captain saw it, too, and ordered the engines slowed, but he made no comment to the young steersman. Anse was grateful for the trust his captain showed. Waiting for the right moment, he spun the wheel hard over and headed for the channel.

*   *   *

Just before sunrise the *Gray Witch* dropped anchor in the Cape Fear River, as close as she could get to the fort. A boat was lowered at once, and Tracy himself accompanied the wounded pilot ashore.

Time seemed to drag. Seamen relaxed and lighted their pipes. The cook served up a good hot breakfast—the first such meal he had been able to prepare since the night they left St. George. After he had eaten, Anse stood by the rail, staring at the fort and wondering how Hobe was faring. He knew that Colonel Lamb must have a good Army surgeon there, but it was still possible that the pilot had lost too much blood. At the thought of that great sharp splinter Anse shuddered.

He turned and looked at the broken funnel and the roofless wheelhouse. With one lucky shot some Yankee gunner had caused them weeks of delay for repairs and had wounded—perhaps killed—one of the best pilots on the coast. It was no wonder Anse felt too bitter to be properly thankful for their escape.

It was nearly noon before the boat came back. Tracy saw the look of worry on Anse's face and wasted no time.

"They say he'll live," he told the boy. "It'll be a long pull, though. We won't be able to move him for quite a spell."

The *Gray Witch* weighed anchor and steamed slowly up the river to quarantine. As soon as she was sighted from the Wilmington docks, distant bells began to ring and whistles to blow. That was the usual greeting for a blockade runner in from a voyage.

The city had changed, even in the few months since Anse first saw it. The patriotic Southern families whose sons and husbands were away at the war made few appearances on the streets. Instead, the town seemed to have been taken over by loud-voiced, flashily dressed people—the profiteers and speculators. They cared little about the Confederate cause. None of them gave a penny to help Lee's ragged soldiers, holding the line at Petersburg and Richmond. They did nothing for the wounded in the makeshift hospitals. All their interest was in making money out of the South's desperate situation.

Greedy men bought the merchandise brought in by many of the blockade runners and held the needed goods to sell at constantly rising prices. The very sight of them filled Anse with disgust.

Tracy felt the same way. When a swarm of speculators crowded around the gangplank waving bundles of paper money, the young captain eyed them coldly.

"Gentlemen," he said, "if I may loosely call you such, there is nothing in my cargo to interest you. No silks or satins or ladies' corsets. No brandies or French wines. What I carry is for the fighting men of the South."

He called four or five dependable seamen to keep the gangplank clear and stalked off through the muttering crowd to report to his agents. As the group began to disperse, Anse was shocked to see that quite a number of them wore neat and spotless gray uniforms. One of the noisiest of the lot was a red-faced major, apparently well along in liquor. It was disheartening to realize that not all soldiers were brave and loyal men.

Seven

The *Gray Witch* was moved north before sundown to a
special pier with a railroad siding. There, under guard of
a detachment of troops, the cases of arms and shoes, the
gunpowder and the food were hoisted out of the hold and
stowed in boxcars. That night they would be jolting up
the line toward the front.

Anse had carefully wrapped the package for his mother
and sisters. Now he went off down the docks in search of a
way to send it. There was no regular mail delivery to the
Outer Banks in those war days, but he had written a brief
letter, which he enclosed in the parcel. After a long hunt
he found a battered fishing boat tied up. It looked
deserted, but the lines and the rig were familiar. From a
Negro dock hand he learned that the owner was in a
nearby barroom.

It was a dingy place, full of tobacco fumes and the smell
of cheap rum. But at one of the tables was a face he knew.

"Hank Midgett!" Anse exclaimed. "What brings you
way down here? Last time I saw you was in Pamlico
Sound."

The bearded man looked up from his drink. "Durn' if
it ain't Anse O'Neal!" he chortled. "Set down, boy. Folks
in Ocracoke'll sho' be glad to hear yo're alive!"

"I wrote 'em," Anse replied. "But I s'pose they never
got my letter."

He went on to tell of the loss of his sloop and his present job. He found that Midgett, who came from Portsmouth, across Ocracoke Inlet on the next island, had sailed south with a load of fish and sold his catch in Wilmington. He planned to start back the next day.

"It's sure lucky I caught you," the boy told him. "I wanted to send this package home to my ma. How's the family makin' out?"

"Tol'able," the fisherman answered with a shrug. "Ain't nobody gittin' fat on the Banks these days, but I reckon they're keepin' alive."

He didn't want to take any money for carrying the package, but Anse insisted on giving him a handful of Confederate bills, worth at least a dollar or two in hard money.

"Tell the folks I'm healthy," he said with a grin. "An' when I do come home, I'll try an' make it up to 'em."

It was dark along the waterfront when he started back to the steamer. Once he thought he heard stealthy footsteps behind him, and he felt nervously the money belt strapped about his waist under his shirt. Gold, in the amount he carried, would be a temptation to any thief. He was glad now that he hadn't shown the belt in the tavern. The bills had been stuffed loose in his pocket.

There were lights and a few roisterers along the street at the middle part of his journey. There he turned once or twice to see if he was followed, but he saw nobody who looked suspicious. Finally he left the lighted area and went on in darkness toward the *Gray Witch,* a hundred yards ahead.

He was walking faster when he heard a sudden thud of running feet close behind. Quickly he whirled about, but the attacker was right upon him. He had a glimpse of a short, thickset man with some kind of club in his hand.

Anse side-stepped as the weapon whistled past his head,

but it caught him a numbing blow on the left arm.

"Help!" he yelled at the top of his voice. Then he was grappling blindly with his heavier assailant. The footpad panted curses as he tried to swing the club again. Anse clung to him like a leech. Desperately he kept a grip on the man's lifted arm with his own right hand, and they swayed and stumbled over the uneven cobbles. Then a crashing fist came up to catch him under the jaw, and he fell through blackness that was shot with stars.

A voice close by was speaking when he returned to consciousness. "Aye, sir," it said. "The lad was set upon by a robber. Young Burns an' me, we heard him holler fer help an' run as quick as we could. He'd been knocked cold afore we reached him. We tried to ketch the thief, but he'd gone tearin' off."

Anse opened his eyes and struggled to sit up. He was on the deck of the steamer, and Mike Rudge and the captain were standing over him.

"Take it easy, O'Neal," said Tracy gently. His hand was on Anse's forehead, and in the lantern light the boy could see a look of relief on his face.

"The waterfront's a poor place for a man to walk alone at night," Tracy said. "Especially a man off a runner, with his pay on him. This town has changed. I remember early in the war when even a lady was perfectly safe down here along the wharves. It's not true any more. Did he get your money?"

Anse's fingers fumbled at his waist. The shirt was unbuttoned, but the heavy belt was still there. His rescuers must have arrived in the nick of time.

"No, sir," he said with an attempt at a grin. "Seems to be all here. The feller sure hit me a hefty wallop, though. My jaw still aches."

*　*　*

For a week there were carpenters and metal workers swarming over the *Gray Witch.* The pilothouse was rebuilt and the funnel patched up with steel plates. Anse carried his duffel ashore and succeeded in finding a small room, which he shared with Donald Burns. Like himself, the young Scot had little interest in going to the waterfront dives where most of the crew spent their time. Instead, the two youngsters took long walks through the better part of town and out into the surrounding country.

Burns was homesick for the misty hills and lochs of his own native land. There was little to remind him of them around Wilmington, but he was fascinated by the strangeness of what he saw. There were live oaks, draped with Spanish moss, flat marshes, and pine woods. He could stand by the hour and watch Negro slaves working in the fields. One of them would lean on his hoe and start a song in a deep, rich baritone voice. The others took up the refrain, keeping the rhythm with their hoes and chanting in harmony.

The words were hard for Donald to understand, but sometimes Anse translated for him as the simple spirituals were sung. The young engineer had read *Uncle Tom's Cabin* and at first he was astonished that the overseers allowed the singing. He had expected to see black-snake whips cracking at the first sound of it.

"I reckon they get pretty near as much work done," Anse explained. "An' it keeps 'em happy."

Sometimes the two young men went to the railroad depot when a train came through from the North. Convalescent soldiers and walking wounded filled the grimy cars. They were coming down from Richmond on their way to their home towns, and most of them were in miserable shape.

A valiant little band of ladies was always on hand to meet the trains. They went through the cars, bringing bandages to dress old wounds, serving fried chicken, cakes, and other dainties from their baskets, and doing their best to cheer up the haggard, suffering men. Donald had the greatest respect for them.

"If the Confederacy wins," he said, "they lassies will hae done their pairt."

While the runner was being refitted, the captain made several trips to Fort Fisher to see his injured pilot. After the third such visit, he arranged with a good woman of the town to take the invalid into her home and nurse him. It was a glad day for Anse when his old friend was brought to Wilmington. That evening he went to see him.

Gaskill lay in the big four-poster bed, a stubble of beard on his gaunt cheeks. Anse had always known him as a husky, broad-shouldered man, and the sight of his wasted frame was shocking. He was little more than a skeleton.

With an effort Hobe managed to smile. "I ain't much to look at, boy," he murmured. "But I'm commencin' to feel a little better. Lucky thing that durn' splinter didn't git closer to my heart. The doc says there's still some pieces of it in me, an' that's what keeps the wound red an' mortified. Ain't got much appetite, but soon as vittles taste a mite better, I reckon I'll git my heft back."

"Sure you will, Hobe," Anse told him. "Does Mrs. Evans feed you all right?"

"Couldn't ask fer more. The skipper sees to it she gits the best. How soon does the runner sail?"

"They're still fixin' her up, an' the moon won't be right fer a spell longer. You ought to be ready by then, Hobe."

The wounded man shook his head. "Not this trip, son. But she'll have a good hand at the wheel. Ain't the cap'n told you about his new pilot?"

"No," Anse replied. "Who is it—anybody I'd know?"

"Could be. But if Tracy ain't talkin', I'd best keep

my trap shut. He'll be tellin' the crew soon enough."

Anse was glum when he left Hobe's bedside. Not only was he worried about his friend's condition and the fact that he wouldn't be sailing with the *Gray Witch* on her next trip, but he also wondered how his own career would be affected. He knew it was Gaskill who had prevailed on the captain to sign him on. Perhaps the new pilot might prefer a different helper at the wheel.

As more time passed and the first of October came, he began to take a more philosophical view. Tracy had been good to him and seemed to like his seamanship. At the lookout post he was sure he was as good as anybody aboard. So he probably wouldn't be dropped from the crew. Mike Rudge was reassuring, too.

"Good sailors ain't as common as some folks think," he told Anse. "An' the skipper's too smart to fergit it."

Moon and tides would be favorable about the eighth of the month, and as that date approached, the runner began to load cotton. All the repairs had been made, and she was as fit for sea as ever. Bale after bale went into the hold, while more was stowed on deck. In addition to the cotton, she would be carrying the usual turpentine and tobacco.

Finally Tracy came aboard, followed by two Negroes bearing a large mirror. It was taken to the captain's cabin aft.

Rudge watched the proceedings and gave Anse a poke in the ribs. "Means trouble, I bet," he said. "The skipper ain't a vain man, so that lookin' glass must be fer a female. We're carryin' lady passengers or I'm a shad. You see if I ain't right."

"What of it?" Anse asked. "Plenty o' folks travel to Bermuda in blockade runners, an' they pay well, too."

"Yeah—but female women's different. They bring bad luck, a lot o' seamen think. You've heared o' Rose Green-how, the famous spy, an' what happened to the ship she was in. That wa'n't but a few weeks back. The *Condor* was as smart a runner as this 'un. She run aground above New Inlet in a high sea, an' this Rose, she was bound she'd git ashore. They put a boat over in the breakers, an' she got in. 'Fore they'd rowed ten strokes, the boat broached to an' swamped. Wal, the rowers saved theirselves, but Rose Greenhow was drownded. You want to know why? When her body washed ashore, she had a forty-pound bag o' gold tied 'round her neck!"

Anse nodded. "I heard about that, but it wasn't her fault the *Condor* hit a shoal. It was just bad steerin'."

"All right, but hol' on, now," said the old tar. "What about that other lady spy—Belle Boyd? She was on her way to Bermuda in the *Greyhound* las' spring. But the gal was late comin' aboard, an' it was daylight 'fore the runner got out clear o' the land. O' course a Yankee cruiser started shellin' her, an' the cap'n had to surrender or be blowed out o' the water. All hands was took prisoner. You can't say *that* wa'n't the woman's fault."

The boy laughed, still unconvinced. "We'll wait an' see," he said. "Seems to me it'd be sort o' fun to have a pretty lady swishin' her petticoats around the deck—if she wasn't a spy, that is."

That evening the captain asked Anse to come to his cabin. When he entered, he was surprised to see not only the mirror attached to the bulkhead but also frilly little curtains at the ports.

"Don't look so scared, O'Neal," said Tracy with a chuckle. "I'm moving into one of the smaller cabins. This is fixed up for a couple o' ladies who'll be traveling with us. A Mrs. Henry Harcom and her daughter."

Abruptly he changed the subject. "How well do you know the charts?" he asked.

Anse was so taken aback that he had to think for a minute. "These along the coast here," he said, "I ought to know pretty well. At the other end, I'm not so sure, but at a pinch I reckon I could find my way in to St. George."

Tracy stroked his chin and nodded. "As you know," he told Anse, "Hobe Gaskill's not going to be able to sail with us for a while. I've looked around for another pilot, but there isn't one I'd trust. Too many good men have been captured. Hobe thinks you could handle the job. What do you say?"

The words made Anse's mouth fall open. "Why—why—I'd be proud to have a go at it," he stammered. "I guess you know I'd do my level best."

The captain seemed to be satisfied. "Can't ask for more," he said. "I'm a pretty fair pilot myself, and I'll be there to help you. You'll be drawing regular pilot's pay—five hundred a round trip. Get your dunnage and stow it in Hobe's cabin, next to Mr. Calhoun's. We'll be sailing tomorrow night."

Anse was fairly walking on air when he went ashore and packed his sea bag. "I'm going to sleep aboard tonight," he told Donald Burns. I know most o' the crew'll be going out on the town for a last fling, but I've got some studying to do."

Finally he had to explain what was in the wind. Donald was almost as pleased at the news as he was himself.

"I'll gang wi' ye," he said. "I can do wi'oot whusky, the nicht."

They carried their duffel aboard, and the Scotch boy sat with Anse in his little cabin, poring over the chart book by the light of a lamp hung in gimbals overhead. It was midnight before they turned in.

Eight

With the final tier of cotton in place on deck, the *Gray Witch* lay low in the water. The fires were started by four in the afternoon, and shortly after that a carriage came spanking over the cobbles. From it descended two beautifully dressed ladies.

"Come on, there, boys," Calhoun ordered. "Look lively an' help with the luggage." And three or four seamen jumped forward with alacrity. Two steamer trunks and a number of large portmanteaus were quickly carried to the cabin. Meanwhile, Tracy was escorting the ladies aboard.

Mrs. Harcom came first—a thin but strikingly handsome woman in her late thirties, Anse guessed. Then he caught a glimpse of the daughter. She was a demure miss of not more than sixteen, pretty as a picture in her pale gray pelisse and flowered bonnet. Brown curls framed her elfin face, and her eyes, under long lashes, were a disturbing violet blue.

That was the last he saw of her that afternoon, but she was still much in his thoughts as he steered the cotton-laden steamer down the river. It weighed heavily on his mind to realize that the safety of such a lovely creature was partly in his hands. He shuddered to think of losing his bearings and piling the vessel up on a shoal—or, worse still, steering into cannon range of a Yankee gunboat.

Tracy had hired a steward for this voyage. He was an

Englishman, pompous and distant as far as the crew was concerned. At six o'clock, when the runner hove to off Smithville, he carried a steaming hot meal aft to the cabin and stayed there to serve it.

Calhoun was in charge of the deck. About sunset he sent off a boat to get the news ashore, and when it returned, Anse heard the report. The blockading line was thinner than usual off the Western Bar, below Fort Caswell. Several craft seemed to have been drawn off in pursuit of a Confederate steamer, trying to make her way in from the north by daylight. A heavy booming of guns from the Fort Fisher batteries confirmed the fact that something was going on around New Inlet.

Almost as soon as the sound of cannonading started, Tracy hurried out. He heard the news from Calhoun and considered a moment. Then he turned to Anse.

"The fleet'll be back here in a couple of hours," he said. "Right now there's plenty of water on the bar, and they won't be expecting us till dark. Let's gamble on that."

He turned to the speaking tube and ordered half speed ahead.

"I'll stay here with you," he told the young pilot. "Here we go."

Anse had navigated the western channel only once before, but he remembered the marks. The course passed several small sandy islands, then ran southwestward, halfway between Fort Caswell and the Bald Head battery on Smith's Island. The bar lay just beyond. Under an overcast sky the sea ahead looked gray and angry, but it was empty of blockaders as far as Anse could see.

He held his breath and steered straight for the line of whitecaps that marked the inlet bar.

"Good enough," said Tracy. "Hold her as she goes." And he called down for more steam.

In a moment they were in the breakers and plowing straight across. The ship pitched and trembled but went over without scraping bottom. Anse knew that Frying Pan Shoals extended five or six miles below the island, so he steered due south.

"Smoke to port!" yelled the lookout. The captain studied the northeastern horizon through his glasses and seemed unperturbed.

"A few gunboats headed this way," he told Anse, "but they're still hull down. May not even have spied us yet. We can be grateful to that fool runner captain who tried to come in this afternoon."

The *Gray Witch* was cutting along at a good fifteen knots now, with spray flying over her turtleback. Once she was well clear of the shoals, Anse swung her nose eastward, squarely into the moist wind. They would be running through weather tonight, he thought. And sure enough, before they were an hour out, rain began to beat against the glass of the wheelhouse. Mike Rudge took the helm while he went to get his supper. Then he came back to steer again. Tracy was no longer there.

It was a lonely job guiding the racing steamer with nothing to share his vigil but the faint light of the binnacle under its hood. The rain still drove against the windows, and he could see nothing of the sea beyond the bow. He hoped there was a good, sharp-eyed sailor aloft, for the responsibility weighed heavily on him.

Suddenly he heard a step, and the door opened at his back. He glanced around, expecting to see Mike Rudge or the mate. Instead, there was a small, slight figure in oilskins standing at his elbow.

"Hello," said a feminine voice. "You looked kind of lonesome, so I thought I'd keep you company."

"Miss—Miss Harcom!" he exclaimed. "You shouldn't be on deck in this weather!"

There was amusement in her laugh. "I'm not made of sugar or salt," she said. "Mother's seasick, and I was tired of being cooped up. So the captain loaned me this waterproof coat. How can you steer when you can't see what's ahead?"

"I just try to keep her on course," he replied. "See—by the compass in that little box. We're s'posed to be headed due east."

"Could I try?" she asked.

With some doubts he let her take the wheel. "Easy, there," he said. "You let her fall off a little. Bring the

spokes over this way. Now look at the compass. That's it—you've got her back where she belongs."

"Well, I declare!" she said happily. "It's easy when you know, isn't it?"

She turned the wheel back to him. "Aren't you mighty young to be a pilot?" she asked. "Tell me about yourself. You don't talk like most folks from the South."

Embarrassed, he gave a brief account of his Outer Banks boyhood and how he came to be aboard the blockade runner. "I ain't—I'm not the reg'lar pilot," he explained. "Hobe Gaskill, he got wounded when a shot hit us on the way in. I'd been sort o' helpin' him, an' the skipper gave me the job."

"What's your name?" she asked. "Mine's Lucy Lee Harcom."

"I'm called Anson O'Neal," he told her. "Anse, for short. There's a heap of us O'Neals along the Banks, Miss —Miss Lucy Lee."

Again she giggled. "That's better, Anse," she said. "I just couldn't go on havin' you call me Miss Harcom. Only you don't have to put in the 'Lee'—even if the general *is* a kissin' cousin. Lucy's enough."

He was glad of the dark that hid his blushes. At that moment a thudding of feet came along the deck.

"Hard aport!" Calhoun yelled. "There's a cruiser dead ahead!"

Instantly Anse spun the wheel, and the *Gray Witch* heeled over, throwing the girl against the side of the pilothouse. He heard her gasp once. Then she spoke, her voice clear and unafraid.

"I'm all right, Anse," she said. "This is exciting, isn't it?"

"Could be a lot more'n that," he told her harshly. "You better be gettin' back to your cabin, Miss Lucy. If they've seen us, there'll be firin' any minute."

Obediently she went down the steps, and he heard the mate hurrying her aft along the rain-drenched deck. Then Rudge came to join him.

"That was a close 'un," growled the old seaman. "Ship wa'n't more'n a cable's length off when the lookout spotted her. Skipper says to keep on this course fer a spell. You want I should take over?"

Anse shook his head. "Give me another couple of hours, an' by then I'll be ready for a nap."

"I seen you had a visitor," Rudge remarked. "Didn't I warn you? Female women's enough to bring trouble any time."

"Aw, pipe down!" the boy told him irritably. "I didn't ask her here—an' she was no bother anyhow. What about that cruiser? Think we shook her?"

"I reckon so. We'd ha' heard from the masthead if she was still anywhere's close."

As if the lookout had overheard him, an urgent hail came from aloft. "Smoke!" called the sailor. "Comin' strong from the port beam!"

Without waiting for orders, Anse spun the wheel and brought the ship to starboard. As she swung over, he heard the heavy *whang* of a swivel gun astern. A shot crashed through the rail amidships and sent bales of cotton flying. Then Tracy appeared from nowhere.

"No harm done," he told Anse calmly. "They don't know they hit us. Bring her head up again, and we'll go due east."

The zigzag maneuver evidently worked, for the next shot flew so wide that its splash couldn't be seen.

"Good steering, O'Neal," the captain said. "You used your head. I think we've passed the second line now and ought to have clear sailing for a bit."

Before midnight the rain slackened somewhat, and the wind shifted into the northeast. When Mike Rudge came to relieve Anse, he warned him to be careful on his way aft.

"That shot messed things up fer fair," he said. "Cotton all over the place. It must ha' hit the bottom tier an' knocked some o' the top bales over into the alleyway. No chance to straighten up in the dark, an' we'll have to wait fer daylight. It's durn' lucky the rain was comin' down so hard. If that cotton had caught afire, they could ha' seen the blaze fer miles."

Anse found the tangle as bad as Mike had said. Twice, in going to his cabin, he had to clamber over bales that blocked the passageway, and there were places where he waded knee-deep through loose, soaked cotton from the bales that had burst. He pulled off his boots and his wet jacket and fell into the bunk, too tired to keep awake for a second.

Calhoun routed him out just before dawn. With a mug of steaming coffee under his belt, he was ready to take his trick at the helm. He found the runner was right on course, and Rudge reported the four hours of his shift had been uneventful. The steamer had logged a hundred and fifty miles since crossing the bar, and most of it was easting.

"Might run acrost a cruiser any time now," the veteran sailor remarked. "This is about where the outside line begins. Jest as soon you was steerin' when we sight one," he added dryly.

The rain had stopped, and they were running through heavy seas and under gray skies. As soon as it grew light enough, the crew was set to work clearing the passage and restacking the cotton. Donald Burns came up from the engine room for a breath of air and stood talking with his friend at the wheel.

"How's your steam?" asked Anse. "We might need a full head in a hurry."

"Dinna fash yersel'," Donald replied with spirit. "We've guid coal, guid boilers, an' the brawest engines frae here to the Firth o' Clyde."

"Not to mention a couple o' braw engineers!" Anse chuckled. "Well, let's hope we won't have to call on 'em."

As soon as Captain Tracy had breakfasted, he came to the wheelhouse. He checked the course and looked at the way the mainmast pennant was blowing.

"Wind's abeam," he said. "We'll hoist sail now. And you'd better bring her over a point to the south'ard. We're in the Gulf Stream current and have to allow for it."

After ordering the sails set, he returned. "You seem to have gained an admirer last night," he commented with a twinkle in his eye. "She talked of little else at breakfast. With her mother still feeling the rough weather, the girl's at a loose end. It's hard to keep her penned up in the cabin. Think you could stand some more of her prattle? I wouldn't suggest it to any of the other seamen, but I think you have the instincts of a gentleman."

"I hope so, sir. Reckon I could stand it fine, just so she don't take my mind off what I have to do."

He tried to act very businesslike when the girl joined him a few minutes later. "Morning, Miss Lucy," he said, eyes straight ahead. "I hope you slept well."

"Very comfortably, thank you," she answered. "And you?"

"Fine—what there was of it. Don't you mind the motion o' the ship? She rolls an' pitches quite a bit in a sea like this."

Lucy laughed. "It doesn't bother me a bit," said she. "I've always been a good sailor—much better than poor Mamma. Have you ever been to England?"

"No, ma'am—never been anywhere much—'cept along the Carolina coast an' Bermuda."

"I sailed to England once when I was a little girl," she

told him. "Mamma has an aunt there—a real countess, with a manor in Surrey and a house in London. We're on our way to visit her now."

"You expect to stay there?" Anse asked. "Or will you be comin' back through the blockade?"

"Oh, we shan't stay but a month or so. We'd like to be home for Christmas. Not that home means so much these days. We've been living in Richmond ever since Daddy went into the army. He's a colonel on General Lee's staff."

"I've heard," he said, "that things are sort o' tough in Richmond. Not enough food for folks to eat sometimes. Aren't you most scared to go back there?"

"No, indeed!" she replied indignantly. "It's our place to be there—close to Daddy. Mamma and I work every day in the hospitals and nurse the soldiers. She got so worn out that our doctor made her take this voyage."

For a little while there was silence in the pilothouse. Both were thinking of the misery in Richmond—Lucy remembering, Anse trying to imagine what it must be like.

"I sure wish the war would end," he said. "I guess you do, too."

"Oh, Anse!" she cried. "How I wish it would! For a few months last year, I was sure we'd whip the Yankees, but after Gettysburg and Vicksburg and Mobile Bay everybody seemed to have doubts. Maybe the best way now will be a truce. When the Democrats throw that horrid Lincoln out in the election, Daddy says they'll make peace."

The young pilot nodded. "I reckon so," he said. "If they've got enough votes to beat him, that is."

"Oh, they're sure to win," she replied airily. "McClellan's the most popular man in the whole North. All we have to do is hang on."

The morning passed quickly, and with all sails set the *Gray Witch* sped along at a handsome clip. Not a smoke cloud appeared around the horizon. At noon Lucy went aft to the cabin for dinner, and Anse turned over the wheel to Mike Rudge. He ate his chow with the crew and lay down on the cotton forward for another brief nap.

About three o'clock he woke with the sun in his eyes. The weather had cleared. Around them the sea was a gorgeous blue, deeper than the azure of the sky. Anse stretched himself luxuriously. He felt lazy and contented.

Then his peace was shattered by a hail from the fore-top. "Sail, ho!" yelled the lookout. "Smoke an' topsails dead ahead!"

Nine

Anse jumped erect on the upper tier of cotton, where he had a good view forward. The distant ship was still hull down but broadside to them, apparently heading northward. From her close-hauled topsails he could see she was tacking against the wind.

Tracy came down from the foremast rigging holding his binoculars. "Take the helm, O'Neal," he ordered. "Keep her on the same course. If they haven't sighted us, fine. If they have, they're working up to get the weather berth."

He moved aft then and told Calhoun to lower the sails. The funnels, too, were telescoped, so that the runner's silhouette was barely twenty feet above the water. It would be almost impossible, Anse thought, for the cruiser to see them at that distance.

As he gripped the wheel, he felt the *Gray Witch* slow to half speed. She still had good steerageway, but hardly a trace of smoke came from the lowered stacks. The captain was standing only a few feet away, and Anse could hear his voice plainly.

"Well, ma'am," he said heartily, "it's good to see you on deck. You're feeling better, I trust?"

"Much better, thanks," Mrs. Harcom replied. Her tones were low and musical. "Did I hear you'd sighted a Yankee ship?" she asked. "How thrilling! I suppose there'll be a chase?"

"It's quite possible," Tracy told her. "If I'm not mistaken, she's our old friend, the *Niphon*—one of the fastest blockade ships in the fleet. And if they've spotted us, I imagine her skipper would give his eyeteeth to overhaul us."

"What?" She laughed. "One little old blockade runner?"

"I don't mean to frighten you, ma'am—the *Gray Witch* can take care of herself. But remember, we're carrying close to half a million dollars' worth o' cotton—the life-blood of the South."

"I see," she answered calmly. "If we were sunk or captured, it would be a great Yankee victory. Tell me, Captain, where's the young man my daughter's been talking about—the pilot, is it? I'd like to meet him."

Anse heard Tracy's chuckle. "He's about six feet away, up there in the wheelhouse," he told her. "Come with me and I'll introduce you."

Tongue-tied with embarrassment, Anse turned a red face toward the lady as she mounted the steps. He could tell that the captain was amused as he made the introduction. Fortunately, he wasn't required to say much. After his mumbled acknowledgement, he could concentrate on the course he was steering.

"It's been nice of you, Mr. O'Neal," she told him, "to give some time to Lucy Lee. I was afraid she'd be bored by the trip. You've made it interesting for her. I mustn't interrupt you any longer at such an important duty, but if we escape the Yankees and reach Bermuda safely, I hope you'll come to dinner with us."

"Yes, ma'am," he managed to say. "Thank you. I'd like to, ma'am."

In the half-dozen minutes that had passed since Mrs. Harcom came on deck, the other ship had continued her northward beat. She was well off the port bow now and still hull down. Anse began to breathe more easily. It looked as if they had slipped past unobserved.

But his feeling of relief didn't last long. There was another hail from the masthead, and the lookout reported the cruiser was coming about. Smoke poured more thickly from her funnels. Some sharp-eyed tar in her crow's nest must have caught a glimpse of the low gray runner, and with the wind in her favor she was coming down now to intercept them.

"All hands to make sail!" Tracy shouted. "Get those stacks up, too, Mr. Calhoun. We're going to need more steam."

He came hurrying to the pilothouse while these orders were being carried out. "Give her another point to the south," he told Anse. "We've got three or four more hours of daylight—time for quite a race."

As soon as the funnels were raised, Tracy called for full steam ahead. The sails were trimmed to a nicety, and the *Gray Witch* fairly leaped through the water. Anse felt her power under him, smooth as the action of a thoroughbred horse. He wasn't surprised when the log was heaved and her speed was reported as a full nineteen knots.

The cruiser loomed bigger now as she swept down from the north. Her bellying topsails were squared to the following wind, and a black belch of smoke drifted ahead of her. Even the upper part of her hull was now in sight, the gun ports open, ready for action.

She was still two miles off when the flying runner crossed her bows. The wind brought Anse the crashing report of a swivel gun, and he saw the spurt of spray where the shot fell, wide and well astern. Then the Federal ship changed course to run parallel with her quarry. Now she could bring her broadside guns to bear, and though they lacked the range of the rifled bow-chaser, they threw heavier shells.

Even at that distance, the thunder of the cannon rattled the glass in the wheelhouse. Anse set his jaw and clutched the spokes, forcing himself to keep his eyes on the compass. It was then that he was startled to find Lucy Lee Harcom standing at his elbow.

"Isn't it wonderful?" she exclaimed. "My, you must be proud of your little ship! We'll run right away from them, won't we?"

Anse gritted his teeth. "Miss Lucy," he said, "you ought to be back in your cabin where you won't get hurt. We aren't out o' their reach yet, an' once those gunners find the range, they could blow this pilothouse right in the ocean."

She laughed. "I do believe, Anse," she said, "you're worried about me. Shucks! I'm not afraid o' cannon. We've heard plenty of 'em in Richmond. But I know I shouldn't be here botherin' you. Good-by for now."

He felt relieved when she had gone. The little ship was getting the most out of her sails and engines, and gradually she pulled ahead of her pursuer. Most of the firing now came from the swivel in the cruiser's bow. Two or three of the shots fell uncomfortably close, but within half an hour they were splashing into the sea astern. The *Gray Witch* simply had too much speed.

When the sun was low in the west and the Yankee a mere smudge of smoke on the horizon behind them, Mike Rudge came to take the helm.

"Skipper's orders," he said. "Wanted me to tell you you rated a rest after a good job."

It was a fine, warm evening, and instead of going to his cabin Anse stretched out on the cotton bales once more. He wasn't sleepy, but the tension of the chase had tired his muscles, and it felt good to relax.

"Anse," said a small voice. Lucy had climbed up on the cotton and sat there beside him. When he looked around at her, she went on with what she had come to say.

"I was showing off, up there in the wheelhouse," she told him. "I reckon you think I'm just a young flibberti-jibbet without sense enough to be scared. Tell me, Anse. How many men have you watched die?"

The question took him by surprise. "I dunno," he said, thinking back. "Two or three, I guess."

She nodded. "I've seen hundreds," she told him soberly. "They bring them to Richmond by the trainload, terribly wounded. Most of the legs and arms have been taken off by the field surgeons, but the stumps are still bleeding. Dozens get gangrene in their wounds. Chest wounds—head wounds—I've seen all kinds. And I've held their hands or written down messages to their folks before they died. Sometimes I've been so miserable I wanted to die myself. Do you understand now?"

"Yes," he answered thoughtfully. "I apologize for chasing you out. You're a brave girl, Miss Lucy."

*　　*　　*

When darkness fell, Tracy had the engines cut down to half speed. Anse heard him talking with MacIvor and gathered that the afternoon dash to escape the cruiser had used up too much coal. If they were lucky enough to sight no more Yankees, they could just about reach Bermuda with the fuel they had. In the first twenty-four hours, the ship had logged three hundred and fifty miles—a remark-ably fast voyage.

The captain joined Anse at the wheel some time before midnight. "With the wind to help us," he told Anse, "we ought to be off St. George well before this time tomorrow, and we won't have to pile on coal to do it. Any time a runner makes the trip in fifty hours, it's something to write in the record books. So just steer fine. The course you've got is right on the nose."

In the morning the weather was still fair, but the breeze was slackening. The sails began to flap uselessly. By ten o'clock they were furled, and the ship moved on, still at half steam. The log dropped from fourteen knots to ten. Anse began worrying about having to enter St. George harbor in the pitch dark and went aft to study the charts.

When six o'clock came, they were still fifty miles from a landfall, with only an hour or so of daylight left. Back at the helm again, Anse heard the sudden hail from the crow's nest.

"Smoke on the port quarter!" the lookout yelled. "Seems to be movin' on the same course we are."

Tracy went up for a look through the glasses. After a few minutes it was plain, even from the wheelhouse, that the other vessel was overhauling them. The captain hurried below to check on the bunkers, and soon Anse felt the quickened beat of the engines. The *Gray Witch* surged forward under a full head of steam. She was keeping her distance now, still out of range of enemy guns.

As he steered, the boy heard a crash of axes and looked aft to see several men breaking up one of the lifeboats while the mate gave the orders. The wood was passed down the hatch, followed by loose cotton from a bale that had broken earlier.

A futile shot or two came after the fleeing runner, but the splashes were far astern. Still they held their speed. Two hours passed, and another bale of fluffy white cotton was opened and fed to the flames.

"Land, ho!" called the lookout. "Right yonder on the port bow."

Anse could breathe more easily at last. He watched the sky line to port and saw the friendly beam of the Gibbs

Hill lighthouse in the gathering dusk. Grudgingly the cruiser astern changed course and moved off to seaward. And with that danger past, the captain ordered the engines cut to half speed once more.

The sun had long since set, but there was still light enough to find the markers off St. David's Head. The leadsmen took their places in the fore chains and began to call the soundings. Tracy stood by to watch while Anse steered. He offered no advice but let the boy pick his own way through the channel. Then they were inside the harbor and dropping anchor.

"Have a boat lowered," the captain told Calhoun. "I'll take the ladies ashore and find out if there's a berth for us at the docks."

He turned to Anse. "O'Neal," he said, "pick a boat's crew and stand by."

Naturally Anse was delighted. It was ten minutes or more before the trunks and bags were brought from the cabin. Then Lucy and her mother appeared. Standing in the boat, Anse helped Mrs. Harcom down the short ladder. Lucy, he was startled to see, was wearing a hoop skirt, and he was worried about what might happen when she descended the side. But she was equal to the occasion. Lifting her hoops in front with one hand, she came down with only a modest flash of petticoat and ankle. Tracy followed, and at Anse's order the rowers gave way with a will. He steered them to a flight of stone steps on the waterfront, where the passengers and luggage were disembarked. Then he left the boat and climbed the stairs after them.

Lucy turned to him with a smile. "We'll probably be here a few days," she said, "waiting for the Liverpool packet. If you get some shore leave, I hope I'll see you. There's no telling yet where we'll be staying, but I'll try to let you know. And be sure you don't forget my mother's invitation to dinner!"

"Yes'm," he said. "I mean—I won't forget. Got to be goin' now or some o' these sailors'll be jumpin' ship."

He touched his cap and sprang away down the stairs. A moment later they were pulling back to the anchored steamer.

Ten

There was no docking space available for the *Gray Witch*
that night or the next day. However, a number of lighters
put out from shore and started unloading her cargo of
cotton. When his duties on board were finished, Anse
spent a few hours on the waterfront. He learned that the
packet from England was due in that day and would probably sail again in less than a week.

There was other news—discouraging news—about the
progress of the war. Before leaving Wilmington, he had
heard that Atlanta had fallen. Sherman's big army was
starting a march southeastward across Georgia, and there
was no large Confederate force in position to stop him.
A New York newspaper proclaimed jubilantly that this
was "the beginning of the end."

Anse wasn't as disheartened as he might have been.
Those same words had been used before, when McClellan
threatened Richmond two years earlier. Then the forces
of General Lee had thrown him back and gone on to new
victories.

At three o'clock in the afternoon, Anse was standing
under an awning in front of a shop when a carriage
came down the street. He recognized the smart turnout—
matched black horses, liveried coachman, and all. It was
the Bournes' carriage, and in it, to his surprise, he saw
Lucy Lee Harcom, sitting grandly alone under her para-
sol. She was looking for him.

"Anse!" she cried, and ordered the driver to stop. "I'm out for a ride," she called. "Come on—get in with me. I was hoping I'd find you."

Fortunately, Anse had on a clean white shirt and freshly pressed ducks. After only a moment's hesitation, he climbed in beside her. The smiling Negro on the box clucked to the team, and they drove on in regal splendor.

"Gosh!" said Anse. "You must be friends o' the Bournes."

"Yes," she said with a laugh. "We're staying at Rose Hill. I thought we might drive over to Ferry Point, along the beach road. Is that all right with you?"

"O' course," he told her. "Any place you say."

He looked around furtively, afraid he might be seen by some of the runner's crew. But if any of them were about, they were busy in the taverns. Once away from the waterfront he relaxed.

"I reckon Rose Hill's a pretty grand place, ain't—isn't it?" he asked. "Lots o' fine company?"

"Yes," she told him. "Handsome young officers from the British Navy and the forts seem to make it their headquarters, and there are parties almost every night."

He caught the twinkle in her eyes and knew that he was being teased. "Don't seem to me I'd fit in so well," he said, shaking his head sadly. "Maybe I'd better make my apologies to your ma an' forget all about comin' to dinner."

"Anse! Don't you dare talk like that! The invitation wasn't to Rose Hill, anyway. We'll have dinner at a hotel, I expect. And I think you're a much more interestin' person than those stupid boys with all their gold braid. You're a Southerner—you're home folks."

Instead of going directly to Ferry Point, they drove eastward first, then north, passing Gates Fort and St. Catherine's Fort, looping back into the edge of the town. A few minutes later they were out on the Ferry Road, running eastward along the high ground. Cozy stone houses nestled among gardens. Gnarled old cedars overhung the white road, and a pleasant evening breeze blew in off the sea.

"It sure is a beautiful kind o' place," said Anse. "Dunno's I'd want to live here always, though."

"Why?" Lucy asked him, curious.

"Reckon it's just too old an' too settled down," he tried to explain. "Maybe it's too British. Our country isn't kept as nice—leastways my part of it. But there's a chance for young folks to do things—to grow as big as it's in 'em to grow. In North Carolina there's no limit to how far a boy can go if he's got the right stuff."

Lucy was silent for a minute. Then she laid her hand on his impulsively. "You keep surprising me, Anse," she said. "I'd never thought it out, but that's exactly how I feel, too. If ever the war is finished, I expect you'll be a big man some day. Like my father."

She looked off over the beaches and the outer reefs. "You wouldn't know about it," she said, "but Daddy started poor, like you. He was a farm boy in the Shenandoah Valley, but he wanted to study law. So he worked his way through the university at Charlottesville. Afterward he started practicing in Staunton and got to be the best lawyer in the upper valley. Mamma was a Randolph —one o' the real blueblood Virginia families. She was brought up on a great big plantation, with hundreds of slaves, but she was in love with Daddy and proud to marry him. When the war began, he was made a captain in the Roanoke Cavalry. Now he's a colonel on Lee's staff. He doesn't fight any more," she added quietly. "You see, he lost an arm at Cemetery Ridge."

It was Anse's turn to be silent. When he spoke, it was from the heart. "I don't wonder you think so much of him," he told her. "I hope I'll have a chance to meet him some time."

That was the first of a number of talks he had with Lucy. They walked together in the old churchyard of St. Peter's, gathered shells on the beach at St. Catherine's, and sailed, once, in a little sloop to St. David's Head. Anse wasn't introduced to the social gatherings at Rose Hill, but on their fourth day in port Mrs. Harcom sent him an invitation to dinner at a quiet old inn, a mile or so from the business section of St. George.

Anse had prepared for the occasion by going to a tailor and being fitted out in a handsome gray broadcloth suit, the first such apparel he had ever owned. It was in the latest style, and when he added a flowing cravat, a new pair of shiny boots, and a long-needed haircut, he made a fine appearance. Tracy restrained a smile when he looked him over.

"O'Neal," he said, "I'd never have believed it. You're a credit to the *Witch*—a real fashion plate! Mind your manners, now, and be sure to impress the ladies. We want 'em for passengers when they come back."

Anse walked to the tavern, going carefully so as not to get dust on his boots. It was after the heat of the day but still so warm that he removed his coat and carried it over his arm. When he was still some distance from the door, he saw the Bourne carriage drive up. The colored footman helped the two ladies down, and they went inside. Hastily Anse put on his coat and straightened his cravat.

He found them waiting for him in the old-fashioned parlor of the inn. When he had bowed over Mrs. Harcom's hand and respectfully greeted her daughter, they were ushered into a large dining room at the rear. It was finished in hewn cedar timbers. Pewter and copper utensils hung, gleaming, on the dark walls, and through the small panes of the leaded glass windows he caught a glimpse of the rose garden.

By the time the turtle soup was served, Mrs. Harcom had put Anse at his ease. Her manner was so simple and friendly that he forgot his awkwardness and talked naturally. She asked him questions about the blockade and the *Gray Witch,* then persuaded him to describe life on the lonely beaches where he had grown up.

"I never got much real schooling," he told her honestly. "Ma taught me to read an' write an' figger, but outside o' that, about all I know is winds an' tides an' fish an' weather."

"Where you lived," she said with a smile, "I imagine those are pretty important things to know. What do you plan to do when the war's over, Anse? Go back to fishing and hauling mail and supplies?"

"No, ma'am, I don't think so. I'd rather stay in bigger ships—maybe learn navigation an' get to be an officer some day. Now I've had a taste o' goin' to sea, I like it."

"Are you sure," Lucy put in, "that you wouldn't miss the excitement—running through cannonfire and all?"

Anse chuckled. "I could give that up," he said, "an' never shed a single tear. The way I feel, I hope this is the last fightin' I see in a long time."

"Amen to that," Mrs. Harcom answered soberly.

It was a delicious dinner, and when they had finished, Anse thanked his hostess with feeling. "I ain't—I haven't had much chance to go out with quality folks," he said, "but you've made me feel right at home."

She took his hand and patted it. "You're a fine boy, Anse," she told him. "We leave for England in two or three days, but I sincerely hope your *Gray Witch* will be here when we come back. Lucy and I would feel quite safe going home in her."

*   *   *

Captain Tracy didn't wait for the packet's departure. He had bought a new lifeboat, patched up the slight damage the runner had suffered on the eastward voyage, and filled the bunkers with hard Welsh coal. As soon as the return cargo was loaded, he would be ready to sail.

On the evening before they left, Anse and Mike Rudge went ashore to do the town. The *Vixen,* another well-known blockade runner, had come in that day, and some of her crew were in a tavern on the waterfront. They were laughing over the story of a stowaway found on their ship.

"We'd poked through the cotton bales 'fore we left," a foremast hand said, "an' never found hide nor hair of him. Then the second mornin' out we seen him come crawlin' out from under a lifeboat. He tells us he's hungry, cool as you please! A long, scrawny, sour-faced cuss, he was. Some of us was itchin' to heave him overboard, but soon as the skipper started bawlin' him out, durn' if he don't come up with five hundred dollars, gold—full passage money!

"Then, o' course, we figgered him fer an army deserter. 'Twa'n't so, though. Had all his papers showin' he was a British citizen—a commission merchant workin' in Richmond. Claimed he wanted to come here to buy stuff fer the gov'ment."

"What did you do with him?" Mike Rudge asked.

"Nothin'. He'd paid his fare, so he jes' walked off the ship."

Mike nudged Anse. "Come on with me," he whispered. "I think I've seen the feller."

When they were outside, he explained. "This mornin'," he said, " 'fore any o' the *Vixen's* crew got shore leave, I noticed a queer-lookin' duck hurryin' into the Yankee consul's office. He acted like he didn't want to be spotted.

Then, just now, afore we went in the tavern, I seen him again. He was carryin' a big bundle an' headin' up over the hill there, back o' town."

"You think he's a spy or something?" asked Anse.

"Why else d'you think he'd stow away?" the old seaman replied. "I say we'd oughta foller him."

They went up the dark street at a fast pace, but the man they were after had too long a lead. He was out of sight when they reached the crest of the hill.

They were well beyond the houses now, and before them lay a rough moor, dotted with cedars and stretching away to the north coast of the island. The night seemed to be extra dark, but there was still enough starlight for them to pick their way among the rocks and trees.

They had gone nearly a mile when Anse's sharp eyes caught a glimpse of shadowy movement ahead. He saw it for only an instant. Then the thing—man or animal—had vanished behind a crag.

"Easy," the boy whispered. "We don't want to make any noise. I think he's down yonder, behind the rocks."

Very quietly they stole nearer. A sound of surf came clearly to their ears, and Anse remembered the beach that lay at the foot of the low cliffs. It wasn't far from where he and Lucy had walked.

When they reached the edge of the crag, they crept forward on hands and knees. Rudge saw the man first. He pointed downward and whispered in Anse's ear.

"Look," he breathed. "He's in between the rocks. An' he's flashin' some kind o' light!"

Anse edged a foot or two nearer and saw it himself. The dark figure crouched in a crevice of the cliff, and in his hands was a huge bull's-eye lantern. By manipulating the shutter, he was sending out a series of long and short flashes with the beam. And from the fort or any other place along the shore, the signals would be invisible.

"What's he sayin'? Can you make it out?" Anse whispered. But Rudge motioned impatiently for silence. After a time the flashing stopped. Then, far out at sea, in the blackness beyond the reefs, they saw an answering light. It flashed only a few times and was hardly more than a pin-point dot. If they hadn't been watching closely, they would probably never have noticed it.

The old sailor pulled back a few feet and cupped his hand to Anse's ear. "He was talkin' to a cruiser," he whispered. "Near as I could make out, he told 'em a Rebel runner was goin' out tomorrer. Said somethin' about guns an' powder, too."

"That's us!" Anse breathed. "The dirty spy!"

Down below them the man seemed to have finished his work. He waited for the lantern to cool off a little, then wrapped it in what looked like a dark cloth. That must be the bundle Mike had noticed earlier.

Tensely they waited for the spy to come past the rocks where they lay. When a minute passed without his appearing, Anse crawled closer for another look and saw him scrambling down the cliff to the beach. He paused there, glancing in both directions, then moved off westward along the sand at a leisurely pace.

Quickly the boy told his companion, and they held a council of war. "I figure he'll come back to town," said Anse, "but he'll likely go round by the Ferry Road. Why don't we head over that way an' lay for him?"

"Good enough," Rudge grunted. "But we don't want to miss him. I'm itchin' to git me hands on the skunk."

They moved along the rocky ridge parallel to the beach and got occasional glimpses of the dark figure on the sand below. After nearly a mile the man turned and started climbing. The rocks were lower here, and he soon came up over the crest, only twenty yards away.

"Now!" whispered the old tar. His short seaman's legs

churned into action as he raced toward the lanky stranger. Anse, younger and taller, was in the lead when the man heard them and leaped away. It was a grueling race over the rough ground, but Anse gained little by little. At last he was near enough to dive through the air and grapple one of the fellow's flying legs. The pair came down with a jarring thud, the black-wrapped lantern hitting the ground yards away.

There was a brief struggle while Anse hung on. Then the man went limp in his grasp. Still wondering what had happened, Anse looked up to see Rudge standing there, spraddle-legged, blowing on the knuckles of his right fist.

"He'll come to arter a while," the grizzled seaman

panted. "It done me heart good to give him a crack in the jaw, though."

Anse got up and dusted himself off. "A nice job, Mike," he said. "D'you mind staying here with him while I go get the skipper? He'll know best what to do with scum like this."

The time, Anse thought, was not much after ten-thirty. He hurried down the hill to the road and was soon in St. George. As he had hoped, Tracy was still up, sitting at a table in the hotel bar with a couple of other captains.

"Well, O'Neal"—he laughed, looking up—"what's the trouble? From the dirt on your face I'd say you'd been in a fight."

"Not much of a one, sir," Anse told him. "But I'd like to speak to you if I can have a minute. I think it's something kind of important."

The captain excused himself and followed the boy to the door. In a low voice Anse told his story.

"Hmm," said Tracy. "Where is he now? You say Rudge is guarding him out there on the moor? I'd better get some kind of cart to put him in and follow you to the place."

Where he found a donkey cart at that time of night, Anse never knew. But within fifteen minutes, the captain was leading the little beast up the road. They turned off on the moor at the spot Anse remembered and soon saw a dim shape ahead. Mike Rudge still stood over his victim, growling a string of imprecations.

"He's awake now, sir," the seaman told Tracy, "but he knows what'll happen if he makes a move. Yon's the lantern he was usin' to signal with."

"You know Morse code?" Tracy asked. "You're constantly surprising me, Rudge. Just what did he tell them with his blinker?"

"About us, sir. What we're carryin' an' when we sail."

"Ah!" The captain stirred the prisoner with his boot. "How about it?" he asked gruffly. "Do you deny it?"

"I'm not saying a word," the man whined. "I want a lawyer, and I'll bring charges against these ruffians!"

"I put some rope in the cart, O'Neal," said Tracy. "Get it and tie him up. Gag him, too. Maybe he can find himself a lawyer in Wilmington, but I doubt it. The way he talks through his nose, I reckon he's a Yankee."

Eleven

There were still some crowds of roisterers in the saloons
along the waterfront, but Anse and Mike drew only a few
laughs as they led the donkey and cart down the cobbled
street. Once a drunken sailor asked what they were carrying.

"Aw," said Rudge disgustedly, "it's on'y a shipmate, too
far gone in his cups. Skipper wants him aboard, ready to
sail tomorrer. Ye want us to take you, too?"

At that the sailor's curiosity left him, and he beat a
hasty retreat. They halted the cart at the gangplank of the
Gray Witch and lugged their captive forward to the brig.
This was a stoutly built compartment next to the forecastle, with a heavy door and one small, barred window.
Until now it had never been used. They locked the
prisoner up, still bound and gagged, as Tracy had ordered.
It wasn't desirable to have him create an outcry in the
middle of the night.

The next morning, with her cargo all stowed and
bunkers filled, the runner steamed out to moorings in the
middle of the harbor. Only then was the spy untied and
given food and drink. He still sputtered his protests and
vowed all kinds of legal action, but the sailors only laughed
at him.

Before sunset Anse was sent ashore in a boat to round
up a few stragglers from the crew. With Mike's help he

soon found all but one or two. He waited as long as he could, hoping Lucy Harcom might come to say good-by. But there was no sign of her. At last he ordered the oarsmen to return to the ship, and preparations were made to put to sea.

The cook had been at work in his galley, and everybody was served a full meal—their last really tasty food till the voyage was over. Anse was too busy conning the charts to do it complete justice. As darkness fell, he went to the wheel. The anchor was heaved and catted. And in the half light of evening the *Gray Witch* steamed slowly out through the channel.

There was a difference in the men's attitude on this trip. Word of the spy's activities had leaked out, and everybody knew they would be hunted. Yet such was their confidence in Tracy's skill that there was no panic. Absolute silence was the rule. No lights showed, and the lookout's vigil was joined by many other watchful eyes along the rail. Even the leadsmen called their soundings in voices hardly above a whisper.

With St. David's Head a mile or two astern, Anse swung the *Gray Witch* southward. Tracy, beside him in the pilothouse, called the engine room for more steam, and the runner picked up speed, slipping through the night like a dark ghost.

It was more than two hours later, when they were well away from the southwest breakers, that a vessel was sighted ahead.

"She's low in the water an' shows no lights," the lookout said. "Less'n half a mile off, but I can just barely make her out. Looks like a runner herself."

The captain went up for a careful look with the night glasses.

"I'd swear," he told Calhoun when he came back to the deck, "that she's the *Lillian*—Captain Dan Martin's ship.

He's a Britisher out o' Liverpool, and he's made some good runs through the blockade. The *Lillian's* built and rigged just like this one ahead—paddle wheels, two stacks, and a freeboard of only four or five feet. But there's no cotton on her decks! I'll wager she's been captured and fitted out with guns!"

At once he told Anse to change course to the southward. As the bow came over, the boy caught his first glimpse of the other vessel—a dim, low shape to starboard. And at that moment the stranger opened fire.

The round shot was well aimed but a little high. It screamed directly overhead, missing the wheelhouse by only a few feet.

"Full steam ahead!" Tracy called down to MacIvor. "And give it to us quick!"

By the time the next gun spoke, the *Gray Witch* was plunging southward at top speed. Anse could afford no time to look over his shoulder. He was steering with complete concentration, holding her steady in the shock of the waves. Two more shots went wide. Then a shell burst close to the mainmast, its fragments tearing through the rigging and knocking a seaman to the deck.

The captain admonished Anse to hold his course and went hurrying aft to look after the wounded man. After that the gunboat's shots flew wild or fell astern. If she was indeed the *Lillian,* Anse figured his own ship was faster by perhaps three or four knots.

When Tracy returned, he confirmed the fact. "I'm sure I was right," he said. "The *Lillian* dropped out o' sight a couple o' months ago, and nobody knew what had became of her. But her skipper never saw the day when he could get better'n fifteen knots out of her. We've left her well astern."

"What about the sailor that got hurt, sir?" Anse asked. "Was it bad?"

"Bad enough. Shrapnel got him in the back and shoulder. I bandaged him up the best I could, but when we reach shore, the surgeon'll have to pick a lot of iron out of him."

Now that the bombardment was over, the *Gray Witch* swung back to her westward course, and, shortly, Mike Rudge came to relieve Anse at the helm.

He spat angrily to leeward and cursed the Yankee spy. "Stinkin' shame we didn't jump him 'fore he had a chance to signal," he growled. "Might ha' saved pore Jackson back there from gettin' hit."

"We're lucky, at that," Anse reminded him. "Suppose that shell had been twenty feet lower. There's two dozen barrels o' gunpowder in the afterhold—sure would ha' blown us sky-high!"

Anse turned in and slept soundly for the next four or five hours. Then he was back at the wheel again. Through what was left of the night, the runner steamed steadily westward unmolested. At dawn some of the men were sent aloft to repair damage in the mainmast rigging, and afterward the blue-gray sails were set. Taking advantage of a southerly breeze, the ship logged a steady fourteen knots throughout the day.

The second night out the young pilot's sleep was disturbed by the groans and screams of the wounded Jackson. He had been placed in a small spare cabin next to the one Anse occupied. Twice the boy got up to see if he could help him, and each time he found Donald Burns there by the sailor's side. Donald had gentle hands and made an excellent nurse. He was doing all he could to ease the man's suffering.

"We can do naught for the puir chap," he murmured. "Wi' a bit of opium he might rest, but the captain says there's nane aboard."

By morning, thirty-six hours out, they had covered

two-thirds of the distance to Cape Fear. Another good day's steaming would put them in position to run the gauntlet under the shelter of darkness. The sky had clouded over now, and the ship drove through occasional spits of rain. If they encountered fog nearer the coast, so much the better.

It was about four in the afternoon when they came in sight of the outer cordon of blockaders. Far off on the gray horizon, the lookout spotted two cruisers—big, fast-looking ships, steaming slowly southward a mile or so apart.

"Give her two points to the north," Tracy told Anse. Then he called the engine room to reduce speed and ordered the sails lowered. For half an hour the runner held the new course, rolling a little to the quartering sea. At the end of that time the cruisers were only blurs of smoke, far away on the port beam.

Anse went off duty at six, so that he could get his rest early and be at the wheel again after twelve. It was a black, heavily overcast night when he returned to the pilothouse.

"Gettin' in close," Mike Rudge told him. "Oughta be in amongst 'em pretty quick."

The *Witch* was running at about twelve knots, her engines throttled back to three-quarter speed. By dead reckoning she was less than forty miles out now, and her nose was pointed a little north of the entrance to the Cape Fear River. But as yet there was no hail from the masthead. By luck they must have slipped through a gap in the outer line of blockaders. That, at least, was what Anse was thinking when he found Tracy at his elbow.

"Steady as you are," the captain whispered. "There's a gunboat not a hundred yards off to starboard."

He turned to the speaking tube and asked for a full head of steam. In the darkness the runner surged rapidly ahead. With no slap of paddles to betray her presence, she soon began to widen the distance between her and the enemy ship. Glancing back, Anse saw a brief glow from the blockader's boiler room and heard the clang of a fire door closing. It was sheer luck that they had missed hitting the Yankee in the dark.

The close shave made him fidgety, and he spent the next hour imagining blacker shapes in the gloom ahead. To make things worse, it had now begun to rain in earnest. The thick drops on the glass blurred his vision, and at last he pulled out the movable sash, preferring to let the rain beat in his face.

If their calculations were right, they were only twenty miles from the coast. The next cordon of gunboats must be right ahead, and Anse peered harder than ever into the wet, stormy blackness. Ten minutes passed, then fifteen, and Tracy came quietly into the wheelhouse beside him.

There was no warning of disaster. The bulk of a ship loomed suddenly out of the dark right in their path. "Hard aport!" the captain whispered. Then, cupping his hand around the tube, he told MacIvor to stop the engines. The runner drifted a few yards, then lay dead in the water.

A heavy silence hung over everything, broken only by the moan of wind and the splash of rain. A voice spoke, not loudly but so near that it seemed to come from right on their own deck.

"How long since you got shore leave, Joe?" it asked.

"Two months an' three days. Too durn' long, the way I see it. A feller sure gets sick o' sea rations."

"Yeah. Oh well, mebbe we'll put into Norfolk next week. I know a little gal there, an' I'll see if she's got a friend for you."

"Shut up, you swabs!" growled a third voice. "No talkin' on watch—that's a standin' order. Good thing there's no Rebs around to hear you."

Slowly the drift carried the runner past the other ship's stern. As soon as they were fifty yards off, Tracy ordered half speed ahead. He turned to Anse with a chuckle.

"I'd have given a hundred dollars," he said, "if I could have answered that Yank bosun back an' got away with it. Bet he'd have jumped clean out of his breeches!"

The night was nearly over when they came within the sound of distant surf. Somehow they had threaded the inner line of blockaders. With the leadsmen reporting four fathoms, Anse swung the *Gray Witch* south for the run down the shore, and before daybreak they were safe under the guns of Fort Fisher.

The usual fanfare of bells and whistles greeted the ship's arrival at Wilmington. And the usual throng of gaudily dressed profiteers was waiting on the dock.

"Vultures!" The captain fumed under his breath. "I'd like to toss a keg o' powder with a short fuse into the middle of 'em."

He ordered half a dozen sturdy seamen to clear a path from the gangplank and led the manacled spy ashore. Anse and Mike Rudge went with him, one on either side. Up the street they marched, with a noisy, curious crowd following, and in a few minutes they reached Confederate Army headquarters at the old court house. A gray-clad sentry barred the entrance.

"I'm Ransome Tracy, commanding the runner *Gray Witch*," the captain explained. "We caught this fellow in Bermuda, signaling to a Yankee cruiser at night. I'd like to turn him over to the authorities."

The sentry called a sergeant, who led the party inside. After waiting a few minutes in an anteroom, they were ushered into a big bare chamber, where a couple of orderlies stood at attention and a bewhiskered major sat behind a desk.

The officer looked up and recognized Tracy. "Ah,

Captain," he said, rising and pushing back a pile of papers. "A good voyage, I trust. Who've you got there?"

Tracy laughed. "I wish I could tell you, Major Dalrymple," he replied. "His papers seem to be missing, but he insisted to me he was a British subject—name o' Smythe-Jones. Trouble is, he's lost his accent, too."

While one of the orderlies took notes, Anse and Mike gave a careful account of how they had first heard about the stowaway, followed him, and watched him flashing the lantern. The tale of the capture came next, and Tracy added his own part of the story.

"The result of his activities," the captain concluded, "was that we were waylaid by a cruiser within thirty miles of the island and were fired on repeatedly. I might add that the enemy ship was the old *Lillian,* captured and re-fitted by the Yankees."

"That's interesting," said the major. He stroked his luxuriant side whiskers. "Seems to me," he went on, "we were warned about a spy who answers this fellow's description."

He hunted through a drawer of the desk and finally came up with a paper. As he read it to himself, his sharp little eyes kept glancing at the prisoner.

"Ah, gentlemen," he said at length, "it would seem to me that these facts fit: 'Age, thirty-eight. Height, six feet, two inches. Weight, about one hundred forty-five. Hair, brown. Eyes, pale blue. Clean-shaven. Long, pointed nose and long face. Speaks with high, nasal voice. May use one of several aliases. Actual name, Ephraim Finch, born Hartford, Connecticut. Wanted for espionage against the Confederate States of America.' "

Mike nudged Anse. "That's him, right enough," he whispered. "Look at the face on him."

The prisoner seemed to have shrunk in size, and his

color had become a sickly gray. The pale eyes darted from side to side like those of a cornered rat.

"Well, Major," said Tracy, "I'm satisfied if you are. I reckon he's all yours."

"Thank you," Dalrymple replied with a bow. "A good job for the Confederacy. I'll send him up to Richmond under guard."

Twelve

The October moon was waxing now, and there would be several weeks of bright nights—a poor time for running the blockade. Tracy was content to wait. There were repairs to be made, and he decided the boilers should be cleaned and the engines overhauled. Meanwhile, he wanted to make a trip south to his old home in Charleston. With Sherman's army burning and pillaging its way to the sea, he knew this might be his last chance to visit his family.

To Anse's surprise and pleasure, the captain invited him to go along. For some reason Tracy had grown increasingly fond of his young pilot.

Before they left, they went to see Hobe Gaskill at Mrs. Evans's boarding house. He had put on a few pounds, though to Anse he still looked shockingly thin and pale. Afterward they talked to the woman who took care of him.

"He's cheerful enough," Mrs. Evans told them. "Doesn't eat as much as I'd like, but he doesn't complain, either. The doctor comes to see him every week. What worries him is that the splinter did some damage to one of Mr. Gaskill's lungs. I hear him coughing sometimes, and I've found blood on the pillowcase."

The captain looked grave and shook his head. "I know you'll do your best for him," he said. "We'll drop in again when we're back from South Carolina. This ought to keep you going." And he gave her a handful of gold coins.

The next morning Anse went aboard his first railroad train. There were two battered old wooden passenger coaches, coupled to a string of freight cars in even worse repair. The wood-burning locomotive was rusty-looking and had been patched in a number of places. The big bell-shaped stack showed half a dozen bullet holes. But it ran.

Jolting over the rough tracks, they pulled out to the west on the Wilmington & Manchester line. Several times they achieved what seemed to Anse the amazing speed of twenty-five miles an hour. There were stops for wood and water and other stops at a few small towns like Whiteville and Chadburn. Occasionally there were stops to repair broken rails.

Late in the afternoon they reached Florence Junction, in South Carolina, where it was necessary to change to a southbound train. Upon inquiring, they were told the next one wouldn't be along until morning. That night they stayed at a bedraggled little hotel near the depot, sleeping together in a lumpy bed. Their breakfast next morning was hominy and a bitter "coffee" made of chicory and acorns, sweetened with blackstrap molasses. And the bill came to twelve hundred dollars in Confederate currency. Travel, Anse thought, must be beyond the means of most Southerners in those days.

They heard the Charleston train whistle and hurried out to board it. This one was no better than the first, but it started on time and chugged on throughout the day. Just before nightfall Tracy nudged his dozing companion and got up to lift their baggage from the overhead rack. Then they were rattling across a long wooden bridge and entering the city.

At the station the captain hired a carriage to take them

out to his old home. Anse stared through the dusk at the imposing buildings they passed, the public parks and gardens. At last the carriage turned in at a huge wrought-iron gate and went up a shell driveway to the house.

Fair Winds was the mansion's name. It stood among moss-hung live oaks, its great white columns shining in the lamplight. A gray-haired old Negro in livery hurried out at the sound of the wheels.

"Marse Ranse!" he cried. "Yo' home agin!"

Tracy laughed and gave him a hug. "Obed, you black rascal, you!" he said. "You're lookin' spry as ever. This is Mr. O'Neal, my pilot. Take his bag up to the yellow room an' mine to my old quarters. Where's your mistress?"

"Mis' Margaret, she comin' right off." Obed chuckled. " 'Fact, hyar she is now."

A slim, pretty woman with shining gray hair appeared at the door. "Ransome!" she called. "Is that really you?"

Anse stood by shyly while the captain embraced his mother. Then he was introduced and welcomed. The young Ocracoker was almost speechless as he took in the elegance of the house and of his own room upstairs. There the candles threw a golden sheen on rugs and draperies, on fine mahogany chests and a great four-poster bed with a yellow silk counterpane.

Luckily he had kept his best clothes in his bag. The dungarees and reefer jacket in which he had traveled were grimy with smoke and cinders. Now he changed quickly, washed at the commode, and ran a comb through his hair. He was presentable when Tracy came to take him down to dinner.

As they descended the curving stairway, a dull, heavy *boom* shook the windows. Tracy smiled. "That's the Swamp Angel," he said. "It's a big Union gun—probably a three-hundred-pounder Parrot—that they fire every few hours. Never seems to do very much damage, though."

There were only the three of them at the long table. The captain's father had died some years before, and his two brothers, who owned plantations on the Sea Islands, were officers in the army—one with Lee, the other with Johnston.

The meal was beautifully served, but it included few delicacies. Charleston had had to tighten its belt in the last year or two.

"Mother," said Tracy, "I've come to take you away, if you're willing. This place won't be safe if Sherman comes here. The Yanks hate South Carolina more than most other states because the war began here."

She smiled at him and shook her head. "This is my home," she said simply. "I came here as a bride. If it's destroyed, I'll save what I can. I doubt if even Sherman allows ladies to be shot."

*　　*　　*

Three days later Anse was on his way north again. It had been exciting to see his first large city, but in a way he would be glad to return to Wilmington. Thanks to the blockade runners, there was plenty to eat there, expensive as the food might be. Also he had had an unhappy feeling about Charleston. For all its loveliness, a sense of doom hung over the place. It could be seen in the faces of old men on the street—there were no young ones left except the soldiers from the harbor forts.

Tracy had used every argument he knew to persuade his mother to leave, but it was no use. Fair Winds had been her home for nearly forty years, and there she would stay. The captain said little as they rumbled northward. He was sad, Anse knew, but there was no more that he could do.

The trains going in this direction were loaded with cotton. The bales looked big and loose, not firmly packed like the ones from the steam presses in Wilmington. They were piled as high as the cars could hold. At little way stations, more cars and more cotton were added till the engine could scarcely pull its load.

"We'll be carrying some o' that to Bermuda," Tracy told Anse. "Maybe the last we'll get out o' South Carolina for a spell."

"You think the Yankees are really coming this way?" the boy asked.

"What's to stop them? Another month or six weeks and Sherman'll take Savannah. Then he'll head north. I hate to think of Mother alone in that big house. The Negro servants'll stick by her—Obed would die before he'd let any harm come to his Mis' Margaret. But if they put the torch to the city—" His voice trailed off. Anse felt very sorry for him.

They reached Wilmington after the usual delays and discomforts. The news from the various fronts was still bad. Privately Anse felt the war could hardly go on very much longer. Little by little the power of the South was being worn away. Every day deserters came furtively through Wilmington, and the military made only half-hearted efforts to stop them. They were scarecrow figures, gaunt with hunger, their clothes in rags. They had endured so much that they no longer cared what happened to them.

In the meantime, the North was able to pour still more men and supplies into the conflict. It seemed certain that if Lincoln should be re-elected, the Yankees would fight on to the bitter end. The last hope of the Confederacy seemed to be that the Northern Democrats would win in November and offer peace terms.

Some of the transient population of Wilmington thought the same way. The speculators and hoarders had grown nervous. Some of them began to let their goods go at a sacrifice. Others tried desperately to convert their deflated paper money into gold or Yankee currency. And the English traders among them were willing to pay unheard-of prices for passage to Bermuda or Nassau.

Several blockade runners took up these offers and set out with their cabins full of such people. It was a risky business, for the weather was clear and the nights were bright with moonlight. Two ships were captured before they could get past Frying Pan Shoals.

At last the work on the *Gray Witch* was finished, and she began to load cotton. After the first of November, the dark nights had begun once more. Anse went to say good-by to Hobe Gaskill, then carried his sea bag aboard the runner, ready to sail at dusk.

It started to rain that afternoon, with gusty winds out of the northeast. They waited for high tide and went out over the New Inlet bar a little after midnight, pitching heavily in the breaking seas. Perhaps the storm had scattered some of the blockaders, for they made their way through the inner line without sighting a ship.

Next morning, some eighty miles out, they were chased by a single cruiser. But the *Witch* had too much speed. After two hours the Federal ship gave up and turned back.

All that day and the second night, the clouds and rain continued. The wind, however, shifted north. That gave the runner a chance to set her sails and make a reach of it to the eastward, saving coal. On the second day, the clouds broke long enough to take a sight. Tracy found their position was three hundred miles west of Bermuda and a little south of the usual course.

"We'll take it easy," he told Anse. "No chance of getting in tonight, so we'll try to make it in daylight tomorrow."

Once more their luck held, for it was noon of the third day before another sail appeared. Then, fifty miles off the Chub Heads, a good-sized Federal cruiser showed up on the horizon to port. The black cloud of smoke from her stacks indicated that she had sighted them and was coming in fast pursuit.

"Full steam ahead," the captain ordered. "Give us all the pressure she'll take."

With the sails still drawing and the steam pushing forty pounds, the *Gray Witch* made her dash. It was beautiful to see her cut the waves. The log line showed eighteen knots—then nineteen—finally a breath-taking twenty! Once again she was proving herself the fastest runner in the Western Ocean.

They soon outdistanced the cruiser. In midafternoon Anse steered past St. David's Head, picked up his markers, and brought the ship slowly through the now familiar channel. This time it was unnecessary to anchor out in the harbor. There was a berth waiting for them at the docks.

As usual, Anse slept aboard that night. His bunk was more comfortable and a great deal cheaper than a hotel room on shore. After the cotton, tobacco, and turpentine had been unloaded the next day, he took a stroll along the waterfront with Donald Burns as his companion.

They had become accustomed to a hospitable reception in St. George. Shopkeepers and dock hands would wave in friendly fashion when sailors came ashore from a runner. But this time there seemed to be a kind of coolness in the air. Donald noticed it, too.

"Ye'd think ablins we had the cholera," he commented with a grin. "Nae doot 'tis the war news has affected their manners."

The Bermudians were ready enough to take solid money, however, and the two young men managed to get a good meal in one of the dockside eating places. Mike Rudge joined them there before they had finished.

"There's Yank sailors struttin' the streets," he grumbled.

"Seems a gunboat put in real open-like an' wanted to coal up. The port authorities is still arguin' whether it's a breach o' neutrality or some such."

The news took Anse by surprise. Ever since the beginning of hostilities, British ports had been barred to warships of either side. But since all their sympathies were with the South, neutrality had been stretched a bit to allow unarmed blockade runners a safe harbor.

"Surely they wouldn't dare attack the *Witch!*" Anse exclaimed. "Not right here in port, anyhow."

The waiter leaned over the table confidentially. "I heard just now," he whispered, "that the Guv'nor's refused the coal. And he's givin' 'em till sunset to clear out or be sunk."

"Good for the Guv'nor!" said Mike. "Come on, lads— let's have a look."

The Union cruiser lay at anchor near the middle of the harbor. She was a long, fast-looking two-stacker, with raked masts like a clipper. But she was equipped with swivel and broadside guns. The flag floating over her stern was the one Anse had been brought up to respect and now had come to hate—the Stars and Stripes.

In the distance aboard her, they heard the shrill notes of a bosun's pipe.

"Callin' back the shore party." Mike translated the sound. "See—here they come now."

A squad of bluejackets, walking in a loose kind of formation, came laughing down the docks. Soon they took their places in a longboat and pulled out to the ship. There was an orderliness about their departure that Anse grudgingly admired. He supposed Navy discipline had something to do with it.

Almost as soon as the sailors had climbed the side, the cruiser weighed anchor. With a couple of short, defiant toots of her steam whistle, she swung slowly around and made for the harbor entrance.

"Humph!" said Mike Rudge sourly. "Prob'ly be layin' fer us when we go out. But anyhow she didn't git her coal."

The townspeople seemed to be a little more cordial after the Yankees left. They had, Anse decided, been waiting to see what kind of stand the government of the islands would take.

The cargo Tracy had expected didn't arrive until the tenth of November, and it was another day before it could be transferred to the hold of the *Gray Witch*. They were almost ready to sail when the blockade runner *Charlotte* steamed into St. George. She was heavily laden with cotton and refugee speculators, but what was more important, she brought news of the Northern election for the presidency. There was no longer hope of a Democratic victory. Abraham Lincoln had been swept into office for another term.

It was a gloomy crew that took the *Gray Witch* out that evening. Knowing that the war would drag on, they had only one task left—to bring the Confederate armies all the help they could. This time it was Enfield rifles, medicines, powder, and lead.

If every runner had carried such a cargo, Anse thought bitterly, Lee's forces might have fought the Yankees on more even terms.

Thirteen

The first night of the trip an extra sharp lookout was kept for the Union cruiser that had come into St. George. However, dawn came without her being seen.

"Looks to me," said Mike Rudge, "like she really was short o' coal. Mebbe she had to sail all the way home to git it."

As they soon discovered, other ships were on hand to take her place. Well before noon, they sighted two large gunboats, heavily armed but slow, approaching on the starboard beam. They never got closer than long range cannon shot, for the slim little runner put on speed and simply walked away from them.

"If that's all the trouble we have," Tracy told his pilot, "we'll be lucky." He went on to confide that he was carrying important letters from Confederate agents in England.

"It would be mighty bad if they fell into the wrong hands," he told Anse. "Once we get into the real blockade, I reckon I'll put 'em in a weighted sack—so we can drop 'em overboard if things get too hot."

The November wind blew cold out of the north, and racing clouds filled the sky that day. Under sail and half-steam, the *Gray Witch* logged a steady twelve or thirteen knots on her westward course. If she kept up that pace, they would be in position to make their final dash during the third night out.

The firemen had little to do that afternoon, but there was no lolling on deck. The breeze was too cold for comfort, and members of the black gang who came up for a breath of air soon went shivering back to the boiler room.

It was toward the end of the second day that more ships came into view. A big cruiser and two smaller gunboats were sighted ahead. Anse changed his course to northward, but the runner had been seen. For the next four hours, until darkness fell, they had to pour on coal and flee for their lives. By eight o'clock they were out of range, and the shells had stopped screaming past. Mike Rudge came to relieve Anse at the wheel.

As the young pilot went aft, he saw Tracy bring a stout canvas bag from his cabin. The captain put a pig of lead in the bottom of the sack and tied the neck tightly. Then he went to the taffrail and made the weighted bag fast there with a strong line. At his order, Calhoun sent a young seaman aft, armed with a hatchet.

"You're to stand right here," Tracy told the sailor. "If it looks as if we might be captured, I'll give you the word, and you'll cut that line. Understand?"

"Aye, sir," the fellow mumbled. His eyes were round with fear, and he handled the hatchet so nervously that Anse tried to reassure him after the captain had gone.

"This your first trip?" he asked, and the youngster nodded.

"Well," said Anse, "you don't need to worry too much. We generally get through without a scratch. Just follow the skipper's orders."

He ate his supper and went to his cabin for a nap before the crucial part of the run. When he took the wheel again, it was nearing midnight, and they were right on the fringe of the inner line of blockaders. The fog Anse had hoped to find was missing. Instead, the wind blew cold from the northeast, and spits of rain were falling.

Visibility was low, but the runner lacked the concealment a fog would have given her.

At two o'clock the lookout sighted several gunboats steaming southward in a slow line, a short distance ahead. Tracy ordered a northerly course, opposite to that of the enemy.

"We're pretty well north as it is," he told Anse. "If they spot us, we may have to duck into Masonboro Inlet."

The boy hoped not. It would mean crossing the shallow bar in high seas and lying inside for a whole day, waiting for a chance to dash out in the dark. To make matters worse, he knew half the blockading squadron would be on watch off the inlet, like cats at a mousehole.

Fortunately, the gunboats failed to sight them. After twenty minutes the *Gray Witch* turned south again and ran as close to the beach as possible without going aground. All the way down the shore, they moved at slow speed, with the leadsmen calling soundings. Most of the time they had no more than three fathoms of water.

The runner had reached a point only six or seven miles north of New Inlet when the same gunboats seen earlier appeared off the port bow. There were four of them, steaming north now, a few hundred yards to windward. In the rainy darkness Anse held his breath. The slow seconds ticked by as the *Gray Witch* inched past. She was almost abreast of the last ship when a yell came across the water. The enemy had sighted her!

"Full speed ahead!" Tracy called to the engine room. As she surged forward, the first guns began to fire, and solid shot came whizzing through the rigging. Then a Drummond flare lit up the sky. Clearly outlined by the light and still in easy range, the runner made a target that could hardly be missed.

A shell burst right over her, driving scraps of metal through the funnels with a frightful clang. The leadsmen were still in the chains, and they called their soundings regardless of the bombardment. Gritting his teeth, Anse watched the white line of surf to starboard and held the wheel steady. Yard by yard, the little Confederate steamer was pulling away from her attackers.

The first Drummond light sputtered out, but another was immediately sent up to replace it. All around the fleeing runner, spouts of spray flew into the air as the firing grew heavier.

"We'll make it!" Tracy shouted through the din. "Haven't had a direct hit yet!"

He spoke too soon. A solid shot from a forty-pounder gun crumpled the hull plates on the port side and smashed through into the engine room with a crash that shook the whole ship. Anse couldn't tell just where it had hit, but he had a sick feeling that someone back there might have been killed.

There was no faltering in the steady beat of the engines. The *Gray Witch* hurried on, less than five miles north of Fort Fisher now. And still the hail of fire fell around her.

"Quarter less three!" called a leadsman, and Anse shifted his grip on the spokes. He had been running too close to the pounding surf. As he bore off, a tremendous explosion almost deafened him, and he felt a sudden stab of pain in his left arm. Half stunned, he still clung to the wheel, more conscious of the lee shore than of his own injury. The first gray of dawn was in the sky. He looked toward the beach and blinked unbelievingly. What he thought he saw was horses galloping. At that moment they pulled up, and a squad of hurrying men unlimbered two cannon. A shot went arching overhead to fall among the attacking gunboats.

Then Tracy was at his side, taking over the wheel. "You've been hit, boy!" he exclaimed with concern. "If

C
BATT. C
102 ND F

you can make it, go and get someone to bandage up that arm. We're all right now. Those are Colonel Lamb's Whitworth guns, and they'll drive the Yankees off."

Groggily Anse lowered himself to the deck and staggered aft past the battered smokestacks. The blood was pouring from his upper arm, and he felt weak and dizzy. Mike Rudge caught him just in time. With quick hands he tore away the sleeve and whipped a tourniquet around the arm above the wound. Then he laid the young pilot down with his head on a coil of rope.

"Take it easy, son," he said. "Them guns from the fort got up here an' saved our bacon. Too bad you had to ketch it, but I ain't surprised. That shell knocked the livin' daylights out o' the wheelhouse. I reckon what cut you was a piece o' glass."

Dimly Anse realized that the firing had stopped. He lapsed into something between sleep and a faint, unconscious of what went on around him.

The next he knew, the runner lay at anchor off Smithville, and it was daylight. Gently he was lifted in strong arms and laid in a boat. The rowers pulled across the river mouth to the landing at Fort Fisher. Then he was carried up a path through the palisades and put on a table in the surgeon's office. As if from a long way off, he heard voices talking.

"A good thing you applied that tourniquet," the doctor said. "He could easily have bled to death. But the wound itself is clean. I'll swab it out with iodine and sew the artery up. With a week's rest and some nourishing food, he ought to be as good as ever."

*　　*　　*

Anse stayed at Fort Fisher for four days. The quarters were rough and plain, but he was well taken care of. For twenty-four hours all he got to eat was hot broth. Then, ravenously hungry, he was allowed more substantial meals.

Tracy came to see him twice, bringing the surgeon gifts of wine and brandy as a token of gratitude. On the second visit the captain was accompanied by Mike Rudge and Donald Burns. Anse had been worried about the young Scot, thinking of the shot that had damaged the engine room. But Burns assured him nobody there was hurt.

"The ship's bein' patched up now," Mike Rudge said. "Lucky thing them smashed hull plates was above the water line or we'd ha' sunk right there."

Tracy laughed. "If you want to talk about luck," he told the old seaman, "you'd better not forget the powder. Ten feet farther aft and we'd all have been blown to glory."

He turned to Anse. "Outside of yourself," he said, "we did have one casualty. That fool youngster with the hatchet cut the line and let the sack of letters fall in the sea. He won't be making any more voyages with us."

Anse was shocked. "You said they were pretty important messages, sir. Any chance they might be washed ashore?"

"Not in a thousand years," Tracy replied. "There was five pounds of lead in the bag. The way things look now, those letters couldn't do much good anyhow."

"You mean the war news is bad, sir?" Anse asked, and the captain nodded soberly.

"Sherman's in front o' Savannah," he replied. "About all that's left o' the Confederacy now is the Carolinas and the lower part o' Virginia. But Lee's still holding out."

On the morning of the fifth day Anse was allowed to travel. Tracy took him to Wilmington in a carriage and put him up at his own hotel. There were more rooms available now. "The rats were leaving the sinking ship," as the captain put it. Only a few die-hard profiteers stayed on in the last of the Confederate ports.

Work on the *Gray Witch* proceeded swiftly. Once more she got a new pilothouse, and her side and funnels were patched with fresh plates. But there would be no more voyages until December. The moon was bright most of the nights now, and the blockade was tighter than ever.

Anse's arm and shoulder still gave him twinges of pain under the bandages, but he was able to go about without trouble. Naturally, one of his first visits was to Hobe Gaskill. He found his old friend sitting up beside a window where he could watch the harbor. He had lost weight again and looked very frail.

"Good to hear an Outer Banks voice!" Hobe told the boy with a grin. "I got word you'd caught it, same as me."

"Not as bad," Anse replied. "Mine was just a deep cut from broken glass. They sure do like to hit that wheelhouse, though."

He went on to tell Hobe about the close call they had had and how the Whitworth guns had come to their rescue.

The older man had an attack of coughing and leaned back after it, haggard and drawn. "Don't seem to be able to shake it off," he panted. "What happened to that Yankee spy you caught the trip before?"

"Well, they didn't hang him, an' I guess I'm just as glad. It was in the Richmond paper. The military court gave him a life sentence in prison."

Anse could see his friend was tired, and he left shortly after that. It was a sad thing to see a strong man so pale and feeble. He wondered how long Hobe could last.

There were frosty nights as December approached, and the people of Wilmington huddled in their houses, trying to keep warm with the scanty supply of firewood. They had reason to be worried, too. Reports from the North told of vast preparations being made to attack the Cape Fear forts and put a stop to blockade running forever.

The only ray of hope came from the fact that General Benjamin "Beast" Butler would be in charge of the operation. He was hated and despised throughout the South for his harsh treatment of occupied New Orleans. But he was also known to be a braggart and a bungler. If his attack proved no more successful than some in the past, it was possible that Fort Fisher, stoutly defended, might come through safely.

There was still time for a voyage to Bermuda before the Yankees were ready to make their attempt. Tracy hurried the workmen to finish repairs and got his cotton loaded by December first. Anse was practically recovered now. He exercised the wounded arm every day and was able to prove to the captain that he was up to making the trip.

They put out on the first dark night, bucking through rain and choppy seas. The usual number of gunboats lay in wait outside the range of the big Fort Fisher batteries, but the *Gray Witch* slipped through the cordon unobserved. By morning she was well offshore and driving along under a gray sky. As he stood at the wheel, Anse's thoughts flew ahead to Bermuda. Lucy Harcom had told him she and her mother expected to be home for Christmas. He wondered if he might find them waiting in St. George. And even though the runner was logging a smart fourteen knots, her speed seemed far too slow to the young pilot.

Suddenly, about ten in the morning, his dreaming was rudely interrupted.

"Smoke dead ahead!" called the man in the crow's nest. "Can't make her out too good, but she's under topsails. Looks like a cruiser."

There was an immediate stir of activity on deck, and the captain climbed the rigging for a look through the glasses. As soon as he descended, he ordered Anse to change course to port.

"She's headed right for us," he said. "We'll try to skirt around her to the northward."

Fourteen

If there was any question whether the cruiser had sighted them, it was quickly settled. Anse saw the larger ship's topsails swing broadside as she shifted her course. The wind was from the northwest, so she would have to run close-hauled. Meanwhile, increasing clouds of smoke poured from her funnels.

Tracy watched the enemy's maneuver with a grin. "Figures she can head us off," he remarked. "May as well let her try for a while."

To Anse's surprise, the captain didn't call for more steam but kept the runner jogging along at thirteen knots. As a consequence, the two ships stayed in the same relative positions, neither one pulling ahead.

"Deck ahoy!" shouted the lookout. "The Yankee's coming about!"

"Good!" said Tracy. "That's what I was waiting for. O'Neal, bring her 'round on a southeast course."

As Anse spun the wheel, the skipper moved to the speaking tube. "Mr. MacIvor," he said, "I want coal dust —all the smoke you can get. But keep your boiler pressure up."

The cruiser was charging down under full steam, now almost within cannon range. But even as she narrowed the distance, the *Gray Witch* began belching clouds of black smoke. Anse was almost choked by the heavy fumes pouring forward over the pilothouse.

"Hold your course," Tracy told him. "With the wind astern, we can stay right in the middle o' the smoke."

They heard the booming report of guns, but none of the cruiser's fire came close enough to be alarming. At the end of a quarter of an hour, the captain called down for more steam. Quickly the runner picked up speed and was soon passing through the forward edge of the drifting smoke.

"Sail, ho!" the man in the foretop called. "She's a long way astern now an' out o' range."

It had been the kind of strategy that Tracy was famous for, and Anse was proud of his captain. He turned over the helm to Mike Rudge an hour or so later.

"Bet you never saw anything slicker'n that in the old Navy," he told his friend.

Rudge grunted. "It was smart enough, I'll admit," he answered. " 'Course, though, we didn't have no way to make smoke in them days. Had to depend on good seamanship."

The rest of the voyage passed without their sighting a single Union ship. They made St. George harbor on the morning of the third day and came to anchor while they waited for a berth at the docks.

Anse hurried ashore in the first boat. He hoped to find the Harcoms in the town, but when he inquired at the packet office, he learned the two ladies had not arrived. The British clerk eyed him speculatively.

"What would your name be, sir?" he asked.

"Anson O'Neal, pilot o' the *Gray Witch*."

"Ah," said the man. "Then I've got a letter for you." And he handed over a bulky envelope with Anse's name on it.

The boy didn't open it till he was back in the privacy of his own cabin. It was from Lucy.

"Dear Anse," she wrote. "I'm sorry to say we've had to

delay our sailing, though we had expected to be on the same ship that bears this letter. Poor Mamma caught a bad cold in this horrid English climate. She just isn't used to so much fog and rain. She's better now, I'm happy to say, and we still hope to reach Richmond in time for Christmas."

She went on to describe several parties and visits to the theater. There seemed to be plenty of dashing young men to squire her about, and Anse gritted his teeth each time she mentioned them. One experience she had had was riding to hounds with the famous Quorn Hunt. That was one of Lucy's accomplishments she had never mentioned, but he supposed that a girl brought up in the Shenandoah Valley would naturally be a horsewoman.

"Both of us are so anxious to get home!" she wrote in conclusion. "The news hasn't been a bit good, and people here seem to think the Confederacy is nearly finished. But that just means Daddy needs us more than ever. So please, Anse, have the *Gray Witch* ready to take us home when we reach Bermuda. Do you know something? I've missed you! As ever, Lucy."

He read the letter through twice and cherished every word, especially the ending. Then he sat down and laboriously wrote a reply to send by the next packet. In it he told Lucy about the last two voyages, the spy incident, and his own wound, of which he made light. The runner would be going back in the next few days, he said, but would probably make another trip to Bermuda later in December.

"I'd feel real bad," he wrote, "if you and your mother took some other ship. None of them would be as safe as ours, the way Captain Tracy handles her."

He mailed his letter that night and saw the big British steamer that carried it set sail next day. Meanwhile, the

Gray Witch had come alongside a pier, and her cotton was being unloaded.

Some of the runners in port were having trouble getting coal. The British authorities had tightened up their regulations now that they felt the end of the war was approaching. Unless a ship's owners had built up substantial cotton credits, the precious Cardiff coal was withheld, for Confederate paper money was no longer accepted.

However, with John Tory Bourne to back his demands, Tracy had no difficulty in filling his bunkers. The *Gray Witch* had already brought out well over a million dollars' worth of cotton. She loaded her usual cargo of arms, ammunition, and foodstuffs and was ready for sea after three days.

Good weather prevailed when they set out, and during the whole voyage only three or four hostile vessels were sighted. The runner escaped them easily and made her way across the New Inlet bar in the good time of fifty-two hours since leaving Bermuda.

At Wilmington they found little cotton available. Transportation on the railroad had largely broken down since Sherman's army reached Savannah, and only a few trains were getting through from the south and west. Meanwhile, more discouraging news arrived. Hood's Confederate forces had been badly beaten and put to rout in front of Nashville. Nothing seemed to go right for the South during those days. The best that could be said was that Lee's lines still held firm around Richmond and Petersburg.

Tracy, Anse knew, was more worried than ever about his mother. Twice he started to go to Charleston again but was turned back because no trains were running south. At last, just after the middle of December, enough cotton had arrived to make several cargoes. Other runners, which had been waiting longer than the *Gray Witch,* gobbled up most of it. But Tracy was able to get four hundred bales and soon had them stowed in the hold. For once, the ship would be making her outbound run without a deckload.

Before they sailed, on the nineteenth of the month, there were rumors flying around Wilmington. It was reliably reported that Ben Butler's army, supported by a big fleet under Admiral Porter, was ready to sail out of Hampton Roads. In another day or so they might be expected off Cape Fear, and there was no time to lose.

Anse's spirits were low as he steered out over the New Inlet bar that night. If Fort Fisher were taken, he knew it would end any hope of returning to Wilmington. Perhaps Lucy and her mother would be forced to stay in Bermuda, far from Colonel Harcom's side. As for himself, he would be stranded in a strange land without a job, while the gallant little steamer rusted at her moorings.

The moon had set, and there was a thin mist over the black water. Hardly had the runner cleared the bar when a low, frightened hail came from the crow's nest. The lookout had sighted a longboat full of Union tars rowing right across their bows. Anse caught a glimpse of it himself then—the boat's white side, the gleam of wet oars, the blank faces of the men.

"Hard aport!" came Tracy's urgent warning. Anse spun the wheel fast and the bow swung over to starboard, but the ship was moving at fourteen knots. By inches she missed cutting the smaller craft in two. There was a sound of splintering oar blades as she swept on into the dark, but the men in the boat were too startled or too scared to cry out. It seemed that their ship must be close at hand, and aboard the *Gray Witch* there were tense moments as the crew waited to be fired on.

Strangely, nothing happened. Not even a rocket flare

was sent up. After ten uneasy minutes the runner was out of danger and racing eastward under full steam.

In many ways that was a miserable voyage. There were no more narrow escapes, but the weather was stormy and the seas rough. The temper of the men aboard was as gloomy as the gray skies. Even the usually cheerful Captain Tracy showed the strain. His orders were sharp and irascible, and he spent a lot of time in his cabin.

Mike Rudge was the only man in the crew who took matters philosophically. "I been on the beach before," he told Anse, "an' prob'ly will be again. Ain't never starved to death yet. Seems like a handy sailorman kin allus git somethin' to do."

It was the twenty-second of December when the storm-tossed little ship made her way wearily through the channel and into St. George harbor. A dozen runners were there before her—the *Owl,* the *Stag,* the *Homing Pigeon,* and the *Charlotte,* among others. But more important, from Anse's point of view, was the presence of a packet ship, recently in from Liverpool.

The young pilot put on clean ducks and a decent jacket before he went ashore. As he was walking toward the shipping office to ask about the Harcoms, he heard his name called in a clear feminine voice.

"Anse—Anse O'Neal!" cried the girl in the carriage. And a moment later she had sprung out and was giving him both her hands.

"Lucy!" he exclaimed. "I hoped you'd be here! I got your letter last trip. Did mine reach you?"

"Yes." She laughed. "It came just before we left. Of *course* we planned to wait for the *Gray Witch.* I don't think Mamma would travel in any other ship."

"How is she now?" he asked.

"Oh, she shook off her cold, but she was seasick all the way across, poor lamb! Now, after two or three days ashore, she's fine again. What's the latest word from North Carolina?"

Anse shook his head sadly. "It's hard to tell," he replied. "The Yankees have sent a big fleet and an army to take Fort Fisher. 'Beast' Butler's in charge o' the expedition. We won't know for a while how it turns out."

Lucy's face fell. "Oh, how awful!" she said. "Does that mean we won't be able to get home?"

"It could," he had to tell her. "But don't give up yet. Maybe Colonel Lamb can hold 'em off. You know Fort Fisher's mighty strong."

"Anse," she said, with an attempt at a smile, "let's not say anything to my mother. I want her to have a happy Christmas. We found a letter from Daddy here when we got off the packet. He must have known about the attack, but he didn't mention it—just said how he missed us and how glad he'd be to see us."

Anse nodded soberly. "You don't think the Bournes'll tell her?" he asked.

"No, I'm sure they won't, but I'll speak to them about it. Mamma asked me to invite you there for Christmas Eve. Will you come?"

He was diffident about it, but he finally accepted, and with that settled, she made him come with her for a drive. She seemed to have put the war news out of her mind, and her mood was happy again. Gaily she described her day of fox-hunting with the Quorn.

"It's lovely hunting country, of course," she said. "Everything's so neat and well-kept. But I must confess I like Virginia better. I don't suppose you've ever done much riding, have you, Anse?"

"Not your kind," he answered with a grin. "But I sort o' grew up on horseback 'round Ocracoke. Guess I never told you about the wild ponies that live on the Outer Banks."

She was interested and wanted to know more.

"They're small horses, really," he said. "Mighty pretty, some of 'em, too. Nobody knows for sure how they got there, but there's hundreds on the island—runnin' wild, like deer. Some folks think Sir Walter Raleigh brought 'em when he landed at Ocracoke a long time ago. More likely they swam ashore after a Spanish ship was wrecked. Anyhow, there they are—the only critters that can live on salt marsh grass an' scratch water out o' the sand with their hoofs.

"The boys an' girls on the island catch 'em an' ride 'em. It used to be quite a sight when we drove the whole herd down to the village an' penned 'em in a stockade. We'd pick out the likely colts an' break 'em to ride—bareback, o' course. There weren't any foxes to hunt, but we'd run races on the beach an' have some real sport."

"I'd love to see them!" Lucy beamed. "Some day perhaps I will."

Their drive took them past the forts and around by the coast to Ferry Point, the same route they had followed once before. Anse asked the coachman to stop the carriage and took Lucy to see the rocks where he and Mike had caught the spy in action. The afternoon sun made it all look very quiet and peaceful, but the girl was impressed. Somewhat to his embarrassment, she put her hand on his arm and told him how brave he was.

The sky was rosy in the west when they returned to St. George and said good-by. Anse went back to the *Gray Witch* with a light heart, his doubts and fears forgotten.

Fifteen

On the evening of December 24, Anse started to spruce
up for the party at the Bournes'. He felt more at ease
about it when he learned that Ransome Tracy was also
invited. The captain looked him over with a critical eye,
helped him tie his cravat, and the two set out for Rose
Hill about dusk.

There were candles in the windows of the big house and
two or three carriages in the drive. A colored butler with
a Bermuda-British accent announced them at the door of
the huge drawing room. Anse made his bow to the lady of
the house and shook hands with the portly Mr. Bourne.
Then they moved on to greet the Harcoms and be introduced to other guests.

It wasn't a very large party, Anse was grateful to see.
There were four or five handsome young officers from the
garrison and an equal number of pretty St. George girls.
With the formalities over, they began to enjoy themselves.
A big cedar Yule log was brought in and placed on the
fire. The young people decorated the room with greens
and poinsettia amid much laughter. Glasses of planter's
punch were served, and then one of the girls took her seat
at the piano. She played well. Soon they were all singing
Christmas carols with gusto.

Later there was dancing, which Anse attempted without
too much success. After two or three dances he and Lucy

went out into the garden for a breath of cool air. They were standing in the lee of a tall rose hedge when they heard voices close by.

"Captain," Mrs. Harcom was saying, "I've read the papers. Do you think the Yankees will succeed in taking Fort Fisher?"

Anse didn't want to eavesdrop, and he started to move away, but Lucy stopped him. She put her finger to her lips.

"We needn't have worried about Mamma," she whispered. "She's known all the time."

Tracy's voice was answering the lady. "Quite likely," he said. "If the fort hasn't fallen already, it's only a matter of time. But we can always make a try."

"I was thinking," said Mrs. Harcom calmly, "that if Wilmington's closed, you might want to go north to Halifax. I've heard it isn't too difficult for ladies to cross the border into the United States. And if we reached Washington, we might get passes through the lines."

They heard Tracy chuckle. "My dear lady," he replied, "I honor your courage, and I've no doubt you'd do it. However, it would be a long, dangerous journey. Why not just leave the matter to me? I promise I'll do my level best to see that you and your daughter reach Richmond."

"Thank you, Captain," she said. "I'm sure we shall feel quite safe in your hands. When do you expect to sail?"

"Probably not for two or three weeks. We should know by then just what the situation is at Cape Fear. And the moon and tides will be right for a run."

Lucy led Anse quietly away at that point. When they got to another part of the garden, she dabbed at her eyes with a bit of handkerchief.

"I'm ashamed of myself," she said. "Here I was trying to protect Mamma, and now I find she's so much braver than I am!"

* * *

The weeks passed swiftly. After Christmas and New Year's were over, the runner crews waited anxiously for news from the mainland. It was the tenth of January when a long, low cotton-laden steamer pulled into the harbor. All the way through the roadstead, her whistle was blaring like mad, and soon half a dozen boats put off to greet her. As she dropped anchor, Anse was one of the first to go up her side.

"Fort Fisher's safe!" the crew yelled. "Ol' Butler's attack was a fizzle!"

Later, in a shoreside tavern, Anse heard the whole story. General Butler, it seemed, had planned to blow up the fort with a giant floating mine. He had taken an old ship, the *Louisiana,* and filled her with three hundred tons of powder. On the night of December 23, a tug had towed her in across the bar and anchored her within two hundred yards of the beach in front of the fort. Then the fuses were lit, and the tug scuttled back out of harm's way.

The great blast went off at a quarter to two in the morning of Christmas Eve. "An' ye know what?" One of the runner's crew chortled. "It was so bad it ack'chally woke up some o' the soldiers that was asleep in the fort! Broke a couple o' windows, too, they say."

After the fiasco of the mineship, Admiral Porter's fleet began bombarding the fort. Thousands of shells fell inside the fortifications, and then several regiments of Butler's forces were rowed ashore. On Christmas Day the defenders were hard pressed. The attack was carried right up to the parapets, and a good many men were killed or wounded on both sides. One Union officer climbed the stockade and captured a Confederate flag that was flying at the top. Farther down the beach, one of the outer works known as Battery Anderson was forced to surrender. Then, just about the time Colonel Lamb thought he might be beaten, Butler had called his troops off! Nobody knew why, but it was a great stroke of luck for the South. Three days afterward the general and his transports sailed away to the north for Fortress Monroe.

All the Rebel sailors in St. George cheered and whooped and celebrated that night. Colonel Lamb and his stout defenders were toasted in gallons of rum. And, one and all, the blockade-running skippers made their plans to sail for Wilmington.

Tracy, Anse discovered, was less elated than some of the other captains. "It was a pretty close thing, from all I hear," he said. "I doubt if Porter'll give up now. His fleet's still there, and all he needs is another general with more sense and more determination. We'll make our run, all right, but it may be the last one."

By January 15, several runners had already left, not bothering to load any cargo but a few luxuries. On the seventeenth John Maffitt's famous *Owl* put out to sea, carrying arms and ammunition. And four hours later, laden with the same kind of supplies, the *Gray Witch* was ready to sail. Lucy and her mother came aboard in midafternoon. They, too, had heard the good news and were happy and confident.

Lucy was in the wheelhouse with Anse when he steered out through the narrow harbor entrance that evening. She had changed from the flowered dress she had worn earlier and put on a white duck sailor's blouse with a blue collar. With the wind blowing her brown curls, he thought she looked prettier than ever.

"Going home!" the girl said ecstatically. "I'm so anxious to see my father, Anse, and I know you'll get us there— you and Captain Tracy."

That night and all next day they steamed under blue, cloudless skies. No mainlander would have dreamed it was January. The air was warm as June there in the Gulf Stream, and the light breeze came from the south.

Not a sail was in sight anywhere around the horizon, and it made Anse uneasy. He thought it likely that all the cruisers had been called in for the attack on the Cape Fear forts. But if the attempt had failed, he wondered why the ships hadn't been sent back to their stations. Certainly they were making things mighty easy for blockade runners.

Late in the third day, as they drew nearer the coast, the wind shifted easterly, and clouds covered the sky. Reminded that it was still winter, Anse wrapped himself in his heavy reef coat, and Lucy went aft to the warmth of the cabin.

There was something strange about the emptiness of the sea that night. Tracy ordered half speed and kept a double lookout aloft. They had reached the area where the outer cordon of blockaders ought to be patrolling, yet there wasn't a sign of a ship.

"Could be some sort of trick," the captain told his pilot. "Anyhow, I don't like the looks of it. We'll wait for daylight and see what's going on."

The steamer pitched heavily in the rising sea, her propellers turning just enough to keep steerageway. At midnight Anse went to his bunk for a brief nap, but he was back in the wheelhouse again by four o'clock. Slowly the *Gray Witch* steamed closer to the low-lying shore, still invisible in the dark.

When the sky began to lighten a little, the foremast lookout hailed the deck. "Smoke!" he called down. "Ahead an' a couple o' points to port—a lot of it. Don't look like a cruiser, though."

Tracy took his binoculars aloft and stayed there in the rigging for several minutes. Off to the west, Anse could see the smoke now. It rose in heavy black clouds above the dunes of the coast. Dimly outlined to the right of it were the fortifications of Fort Fisher. With a sinking heart he knew that the dark cloud came from Fort Caswell, on the opposite side of the main channel.

At that moment Tracy returned to the pilothouse. "It's Caswell that's burning," he said gloomily. "But there's a ship headed this way, too. I don't think she's a gunboat. Might be a runner, trying to get away."

He kept the glasses on the approaching craft, now more plainly seen as the light increased. "Yes, sir, by George!" he cried. "That's Maffitt's *Owl* that sailed out ahead of us. Put your helm over and we'll hail her."

He called to Calhoun to run up the Confederate flag. The other vessel was moving fast, but she changed course as soon as the Stars and Bars showed at the main peak. Within three or four minutes the *Gray Witch* swept up alongside her. The brown-bearded Maffitt waved to Tracy and called across the choppy water.

"Stay clear o' the Cape Fear!" he warned. "They've taken the forts. The whole blockade fleet's lying inside Fisher's Island waiting for stray runners like us. Four of 'em were captured yesterday. I just got away by the skin o' my teeth."

"Where you headed now, John?" Tracy asked.

"I've got to make a try at Charleston. If we can't get in there, then back to Bermuda—and England. Better come with us, Ranse."

"Sorry," Tracy replied. "I've got passengers that have to reach Richmond. We'll try somewhere else. Good luck, John!"

Maffitt shook his head as if in pity. But before he could say anything more, the lookouts on both runners let out a yell.

"Gunboats!" they cried in chorus. "Three—no, four of 'em—comin' out past the island!"

"Full speed ahead," Tracy ordered. And as the two captains waved farewell, the *Owl* and the *Gray Witch* pulled rapidly apart.

At his skipper's command, Anse put the helm over on a northward course, skirting Frying Pan Shoals. The *Owl*, meanwhile, headed south on her way to Charleston.

Long before the Yankee ships could round the shoals, the *Gray Witch* was well up the coast off the ruins of Fort Fisher. But there, just after they passed New Inlet, they caught sight of more Federal gunboats roaring out across the bar. It looked as if orders had been issued to sink or capture the fast little runner.

There was plenty of coal in the bunkers—enough even to take them to Halifax, if that was Tracy's destination. Anse fully expected him to lay a new course eastward, around Cape Lookout and Cape Hatteras, but instead the captain went aft, leaving him in charge. The pursuers had never come within cannon range. Now they were dropping steadily astern.

As the runner drew abreast of Masonboro Inlet, Lucy climbed the wheelhouse steps. She was dressed as he had seen her first, when she came aboard in Wilmington.

"Anse," she said, "tell me what's wrong. Shouldn't we be in the river by now?"

He saw her worried frown and realized she must have been dressing in her cabin when they met the *Owl*.

"Gosh, Miss Lucy," he said. "Didn't anybody tell you? Things aren't so good. Fort Fisher's been captured, an' the river's full o' Yankees. I don't know where we're goin' now, but the skipper told me to head north."

He had seen the shock in Lucy's face. Now it cleared. Her eyes flashed. "So that's it!" she exclaimed. "No wonder Captain Tracy's gone in to talk to Mamma. What do *you* think we should do, Anse?"

He took a moment to think it over. "Well," he said, "I

know most o' the bars an' inlets along the shore. Maybe we could put in somewhere if we get hard pressed.''

"I think that's a splendid idea," she told him. "I'm going to talk to the captain." And before he could stop her, she was hurrying aft along the deck.

Within five minutes she was back, and Tracy was with her.

"What's this about inlets?" he asked brusquely.

"Nothing much, sir," Anse told him. "I was just thinkin' it's a long ways to Nova Scotia, an' General Lee won't get any good of our cargo if we go there."

"So?" the captain prompted.

"Well, if we could get inside, some place where the Yankees haven't landed yet, maybe we could put the guns an' passengers ashore. New River Inlet's patrolled. I know that 'cause my sloop was shot up there. I reckon it's the same at Beaufort. But Bogue Inlet might be open. An' there's one other that's real handy—Topsail Inlet—right over yonder off the port bow."

Hardly were the words out of his mouth when a hail came from the lookout. "Smoke to the nor'east!" he called. "Looks like three ships, all headed this way!"

Tracy rubbed his chin and made a quick decision. "Take her in," he said. "If we can make it through the inlet before they sight us, we've got a chance."

The order thrilled Anse, but it scared him, too. As he spun the wheel over, he was wondering how much water he would find on the bar. Also he realized with dread that the Federal forces might already have come overland to occupy the inner shore.

"You'll need soundings," said Tracy, and at once he sent leadsmen to the fore chains.

The breakers were close now. Anse set his jaw and gripped the spokes hard.

"Mark three!" came the singsong call. "Quarter less three!"

The steamer had cut down her speed, but the white surf on the bar seemed to come closer at a frightening pace. When the leadsman called a quarter less twain, Anse breathed a prayer. That meant only about ten feet of water, and they drew eight. If they could have waited for high tide, it wouldn't have been so bad. But the gunboats off to starboard were approaching fast.

Now the *Gray Witch* was right among the breakers. Her bottom struck sand and threw Anse against the wheel with a sickening lurch. Then he felt the vessel slide forward on the next wave. Twice more she scraped the bar and twice pulled free. The last time her propellers thrashed, half out of water, but still she inched forward.

"Mark three!" yelled one of the leadsmen jubilantly. She was over!

A marshy point of land lay ahead, directly opposite Topsail Inlet, but Anse knew there was a cove behind it. He headed for the entrance to this little bay, steering by instinct, since there were no buoys or markers. As he had guessed, the channel lay to the left, and though the soundings showed only about twelve feet of water, the runner moved on without mishap.

Not a sign of human life was to be seen there in the narrow sound. There wasn't a house or even a fisherman's skiff. Only the gulls and terns flew screaming overhead. Anse rounded the sandy point and swung northward into the cove, where dunes and tall bulrushes hid the vessel from the sea. Then he drew a long breath of relief and turned to Tracy with a grin.

"Here we are, sir," he said. "An' there isn't a Yankee around. If you want, we could anchor here an' take a boat up past the bend o' the creek. There's a few houses there, an' I could find out how things stand."

The captain clapped him on the back. "You've done a fine job, O'Neal," he said. "I won't forget it. How many men do you want in the boat?"

"I thought I'd just take the dinghy an' row myself," said Anse. "Some o' the folks there may remember me."

Sixteen

On the way to his cabin he met Lucy by the companion-way. Her face was radiant.

"I knew you were wonderful, Anse," she said. "And now I reckon Captain Tracy knows it, too!"

"Let's wait a bit," he warned her. "Could be there's Yankee troops quartered up there. That's why I aim to put on my oldest clothes an' try to act like a plain fisherman."

He found a torn shirt and a pair of ragged, faded old dungarees. Going barefooted would have given an added touch to his disguise, but the weather was cold, and he knew even the poorest fisherman would wear sea boots in January.

Two other sailors lowered the dinghy, and Anse got in. The tide had started to flood, so he had the current with him. Rowing easily, he reached the bend in half an hour and went around it to his left. The water, he observed, was fairly deep in the channel. With luck he thought the steamer could come up this far.

Perhaps a dozen houses formed the little village on the right bank. There was a general store there, he recalled, and a tiny church. Two or three long ramshackle piers reached out into the water. He tied up at one of these and hailed a ten-year-old boy who sat there fishing.

"Catchin' anything?" he asked.

"On'y a couple o' crabs," the lad replied.

"Tell me," Anse pursued, "you seen any Yankee gunboats up this way?"

The boy shook his head. "Ain't bothered us none. They's been some Yank soldiers over 'round Scott's Hill, though. That's a ways west o' here."

Anse went on up the pier and stopped at the little store. The storekeeper was an elderly man, and two others, even older, sat next to the potbellied stove. Anse made a small purchase of fishing line while he watched the oldsters and listened to their conversation. They talked gloomily about the war and the way the army was pinned down at Petersburg.

When he was sure where their sympathies lay, Anse broke into the talk. "You reckon folks 'round here would like to do somethin' that might help General Lee?" he asked.

They eyed him suspiciously, as they would any stranger.

"Don't remember me, do you?" He chuckled. "I was in here last year—sailin' the supply boat. Now I'm on a blockade runner. She's lyin' down the cove a way, loaded with guns an' ammunition. Now that the Yanks have captured Fort Fisher, we had to come in through Topsail Inlet. But if we could land here an' load the cargo into wagons, we might be able to take it across country to the railroad."

The old fellows held a whispered consultation. "By gollies!" one of them said at last. "It ain't a bad idee! At high tide they's nigh ten foot o' water right up to the dock. You go fetch yore steamer whilst we round up some wagons."

"When's high water?" asked Anse.

"A couple of hours later'n it is on the bar. Say four o'clock this afternoon. That'll give us enough time to git ready. 'Tain't hardly noon yit."

Anse was well pleased with his morning's work. Even before he left the dock he saw the three old men hurrying off up the road with surprising agility. He rowed back the way he had come, testing the depth of the water with an oar as he went. The tide was coming in fast now, and he was sure the channel would be deep enough for the steamer.

They were waiting anxiously on deck for his return. From the crow's nest a lookout had been able to get a glimpse of the inlet to the south and reported a Federal gunboat was anchored off the bar.

"We don't know yet," Tracy told Anse, "whether the Yanks saw us or not. We've just been afraid they might try to follow us in at high tide. How'd you make out up there?"

Anse described the situation. "They're scouring 'round to find some wagons right now," he said. "Tide'll be full in about four hours. There's 'most enough water already."

He ate his noon meal on deck, though he was too excited to be very hungry. An hour later Tracy went up the rigging to reconnoiter. Studying the blockader through the glasses, he found no signs of activity, even though the tide must be nearing the full on the bar. He left word with the lookout to hail him immediately if the gunboat bestirred herself. Then he came down to talk to Anse.

"Hard to tell whether she knows we're here," he said. "If she starts in after us, we'll have to cut it pretty fine. Maybe we can't even wait for flood tide. Think you can find your way up there without running us aground?"

"I can try," Anse replied. "We'll just have to go slow an' take soundings all the way."

He took his post at the wheel, and the anchor was raised. The tide had swung the steamer's stern upstream. Now he had to turn her in little more than her own length. By reversing one screw and driving with the other, the *Gray Witch* was brought slowly about and started up the creek. At the bend the leadsman called a reading of under two fathoms, but Anse kept to the channel and got around safely. The fishing hamlet was now only half a mile away.

Anse began to feel the strain. He wiped the sweat off his hands on his ragged pants and steered with frowning concentration. At the end of the pier stood the youngster he had talked to earlier. The lad was waving his arms and pointing out into the creek. There Anse saw a floating keg that hadn't been there before. It must be a buoy, placed for his guidance, and he bore over to port to pass it on the starboard side. The soundings at that point still showed a bare ten feet of water.

Very carefully he edged the runner in till her side was only yards from the end of the rickety dock. The engines were stopped, and Mike Rudge heaved a line to the waiting boy, who quickly threw a hitch around one of the pilings. A moment later Tracy sprang ashore.

Anse relaxed and unbent stiff fingers from around the spokes. It had been a ticklish piece of steering, and he was glad it was over. Lucy came to join him in the wheelhouse.

"I didn't want to bother you before," she said, "so I stayed out of the way. Look, Anse! What's that dust up the road?"

Along the sandy track, he could see some kind of procession moving. Through the dust clouds, as it came nearer, the long ears of mules were visible and the heads of people, walking beside them.

"It's the wagons!" he cried. "I sure hope they got enough to do some good!"

The little caravan pulled up in front of the store, not far from the dock. There were, Anse could now count, six wagons in all, each drawn by a pair of mules or horses. They were dingy, unpainted farm vehicles of the kind used for hauling hay, tobacco, and cotton, but they looked wonderful to the young pilot.

Tracy was talking to the little group of old men, women, and boys who accompanied the wagons. Now he hurried down to the steamer, a broad grin on his face.

"Come on there, men," he ordered. "Open up those hatches. Calhoun, see how fast you can get 'em to hoist the cargo out."

While the cases of rifles were being removed from the hold, Anse went up to the wagons. The old codger who had first agreed to his idea was sitting on the porch of the store, mopping his brow.

"We got 'em fer ye, son!" he announced proudly. "Had to scour a heap o' territory fust, but they're here. Ye see they's nothin' 'round this neck o' the woods but leetle farms an' fishermen. On'y one big plantation, an' the Yank foragers done made off with all the livestock there. As fer the slaves, they jes' plumb took to their heels, soon as the bluecoats hove in sight. But y'all are welcome to these wagons, an' the young 'uns here'll go along to fetch 'em back."

Anse inquired about the condition of the roads and the best route to follow if they were to avoid Yankee patrols. He had no map to guide him, but he knew the Weldon Railroad line, running north to Goldsboro and Petersburg, must be within fifteen or twenty miles.

"I reckon the place ye'd oughta head fer is Rocky P'int," the old storekeeper told him. "Last I heered, Bragg had some Confed'rit cavalry thar, pertectin' the railroad. Ye'd hev to cross the northeast branch o' the Cape Fear, but the bridge is prob'ly still open."

Tracy looked over the wagons, making sure they were strong enough to hold the heavy loads they would have to carry. Then the crew began putting the rifles, lead, and powder into the stout wagon boxes. It was sunset by the time the loading was finished.

"Ladies," the captain told the Harcoms, "you'll ride with me on the lead wagon. I'm going to let O'Neal scout ahead, so we'll have warning if we run into any Federals. First of all, though, we'll have supper aboard the steamer. Then we'll start as soon as it's dark."

"Sir," said Anse, "I'd like to cut some o' that marsh hay to cover the loads in the wagons. Could I have some o' the crew to help?"

Tracy agreed and detailed half a dozen seamen to the task. Within half an hour, they had cut enough marsh grass to disguise the cases and kegs. Then Anse ate a hasty meal and mounted an old brown mule. The drivers were already assembling at the wagons, and Lucy and her mother had climbed to the seat of the first one. The girl waved cheerfully.

"Good luck, Anse," she called. "We'll see you soon."

The crew, under Calhoun's command, would stay with the *Gray Witch*. Their orders were to take her back to her morning's anchorage and keep her hidden as well as they could. If Union gunboats attacked, they were to beach and burn the vessel.

In the dusk Anse rode out of the hamlet and took the sandy track westward over the dunes. Behind him, in the distance, he could see the wagon teams toiling upward, with villagers helping at the wheels. His heart warmed at the eagerness of these poor people to help the forlorn cause of the South.

The mule was slow but willing. It plodded steadily along what was now a better road, leading over flat country between patches of woods and small, scattered farms. It was a lonely place. No lights shone from the cabins. Somewhere off in the pines a dog howled mournfully, and nearer at hand an owl gave its quavering call.

After an hour Anse saw a small town ahead. He rode slowly toward the first of the houses, watching for any sign of troops, but the street lay deserted. A dim light came from the tavern, and he dismounted at the hitching rail to reconnoiter. Through the dusty window, he could see two old men playing checkers, while a gloomy-looking fellow in an apron polished glasses behind the bar. He was pretty certain that if soldiers were in the neighborhood, some of them would have come to the tavern. He remounted the mule and rode back to wait for the wagons.

After fifteen or twenty minutes they hove in sight, moving at a slow walk. Tracy halted the train when he saw his scout.

"Looks all right," Anse reported in low tones. "Quiet enough, anyhow. Let me talk to one o' the boy drivers back there, an' see if there's any way around the town. If we go on through, it might raise a little commotion."

One of the youngsters told him the place was called Hampstead. "Thar's a road we passed, a piece back," he went on. "It'd take us 'round to the north an' we'd miss the town. I reckon we could find our way back to the main road afterwards."

Anse consulted with the captain, and the caravan turned around. They found the byroad without much difficulty. It wasn't as good as the one they had been on, but aside from a small hill or two and a stream that had to be forded, it was passable. Some time after midnight, they were well past Hampstead and back on the main road once more.

Riding on ahead, Anse came to an old plantation that seemed to stand deserted. The big house loomed dark and forbidding, its four white columns ghostly in the night. When he rode nearer, he could see the windows were broken and the front door gaping open.

A driveway led around to the back, where he found empty stables and dilapidated slave quarters, no longer lived in. There was also a huge old tobacco barn. He returned to the road, dismounted, and stretched his legs, cramped with the cold. The weary mule closed its eyes and dozed patiently with its head hanging down.

After what seemed a long time, the creaking of the wagons could be heard. Anse went out and waited till they pulled abreast of him. He felt a pang of pity for Lucy and her mother, huddled against each other and trying to sleep on the hard, jolting board that formed the seat.

"Teams are tired," Tracy said. "We'll have to find a place to rest, where we won't be seen."

"Maybe this'll do, sir," Anse told him. "Back yonder there's a tobacco barn big enough to hide all the wagons. Not a soul around, far's I can see. I reckon the white folks left quite a while back, an' the Negroes just skedaddled."

The captain climbed stiffly down and went to look for himself.

"Good enough," he said when he returned. "We can stay in there all day without being spotted an' start again after dark. You'd better get some rest yourself, so you can scout ahead in daylight and see how much farther we have to go."

Anse opened the barn doors wide, and the six wagons were driven inside. The dark interior was redolent of the smell of cured tobacco, but the floor was empty now. They brought in armfuls of hay, on which the ladies could sleep. Then the teams were unharnessed and fed, and everybody lay down. For a few minutes, Anse worried about the rest of the trip. Then, before he knew it, he was dreaming.

Seventeen

It was nearly ten o'clock of a gray, cloudy morning when Anse woke up. In the gloomy interior of the barn the others were already stirring. The horses and mules munched steadily at their fodder, and the drivers were eating such cold rations as they had brought along. A cooking fire in the dry old barn would have been too risky.

Lucy saw Anse sit up and brought him some bread and cheese for his breakfast. Water had been carried in from the plantation well sometime before dawn.

After he had washed and eaten, Anse had a talk with the oldest of the boys. "How much further do you reckon it is to the bridge across the river?" he asked.

The youngster scratched his head. "I ain't sure," he replied, "but not more'n two-three hours walkin', I'd say. All's I know is, we're on the right road."

"I'll go ahead an' have a look," Anse told him. "How about lettin' me wear your hat?"

The boy was proud to lend his headgear—a battered old broad-brimmed felt, covered with dust and hayseed. When he put it on, Anse knew he looked the part of a real country bumpkin.

He roused the old mule and mounted bareback. "I'll see how the land lies, sir," he told Tracy. "An' I'll try to be back 'fore dark."

They opened the barn door wide enough for him to
ride out and closed it again after him. A few minutes later
he was plodding up the road, slouched on the mule's bony
back.

The road seemed strangely deserted. In an hour's ride,
covering perhaps three miles, he met only one other traveler,
a gray-haired old Negro man leading a cow. The man
watched his approach with scared eyes, but once he got a
closer look at Anse, his fears appeared to leave him. "Mo'-
nin', massa," he mumbled, and touched his grizzled fore-
lock.

Anse went on, wondering what had become of all the
inhabitants of the region. Something must have happened,
he thought, to keep them off the highway. Ten minutes
later he found his anwser.

He saw a straggling group of blue-clad soldiers moving up
a lane on his left. They were still a quarter of a mile away
as they approached the road he was on. His first impulse
was to turn the mule and make off into the woods, but
after a moment's hesitation he rode on.

There were fifteen or twenty men in the platoon, but
they sauntered along in no particular formation. As he
drew closer, he saw that some of them carried burlap bags
in addition to their rifles and knapsacks. Their uniforms
looked wrinkled and dusty.

At the junction of the lane with the main road they
stopped, threw down their accoutrements, and built a
small fire on which they started to boil coffee. Anse rode
slowly toward them, whistling to keep up his courage.

A sentry stepped out in front of him, rifle at the ready.
"Halt!" he ordered gruffly. "Where you headed, young
feller?"

Anse grinned at him stupidly. "Who—me?" he asked.
"Ain't headed no place—on'y home. Up the road yonder a
piece."

"Well," growled the soldier, "where you been then?"

Anse stared, trying to look as half-witted as possible. "Jes' down to ole Miz Hawkins," he whined. "Ma done sent her some aigs. Pore soul ain't got hardly nothin' to eat."

A fat sergeant had been listening to the interrogation. Now he got up and shambled nearer. "So!" he remarked craftily. "Your mother's got some chickens, has she?"

"Did have, this mawnin'," the boy replied. "Don' reckon they's any of 'em lef' now, though."

"Whadda ya mean by that?" the sergeant demanded with a scowl.

"Jes' as I come out," Anse told him, "I seed a passel o' Gin'l Bragg's hoss soldiers ridin' down the road. They sho' like chicken meat."

The sergeant looked startled. "Cavalry, you say? How many of 'em?"

"I dunno," Anse replied, frowning over the problem. "More'n I could count on my fingers, anyways."

"And they're headed this way?"

"Wal—last I seed 'em they was."

The sergeant turned back to the lolling platoon. "Come on, there!" he shouted. "Pick up your gear an' get organized. We'll git out o' here in a hurry!"

Anse still wore his stupid grin as he watched the bluecoats go hurrying away down the lane. Not till they were hidden by the woods did he kick the mule into motion again.

"I sure hope"—he chuckled to himself—"that 'ole Miz Hawkins' gets some nourishment out o' those eggs!"

He rode on another three miles and started downhill into a valley. The northeast branch of the Cape Fear was a wide river below him. And there, at the foot of the hill, was the plank bridge that led across it. That wasn't all he saw, however. Many horses were tethered to the rail at the

nearer end of the bridge, and their riders—men in non-
descript gray—were spread out in a skirmish line around
the bridgehead.

"Golly!" thought Anse in amazement. "I wasn't really
lying to those Yanks at all!"

He gave the mule another dig with his heels and went
down the hill at an ambling trot. This time there was no
need to play a part when he was challenged. Within
minutes he had explained the situation to the youthful
lieutenant who commanded the detail.

"So we've got six wagonloads o' rifles an' ammunition
back there," he concluded, "an' two ladies on their way to
Richmond. If you could give us an escort, we could travel
by daylight."

The young officer rubbed his chin. "We heard there

were Union foragers over this way," he replied, "and we're here to keep 'em from crossing the bridge. How many men in the bunch you saw?"

"I counted eighteen," Anse told him. "But they hightailed it south in a hurry when I mentioned Confederate cavalry."

The lieutenant laughed. "Well," he said, "I reckon I don't have to send back for orders in a case like this. I can spare ten men to ride with you, and if you can bring the wagons here by four o'clock, there ought to be a train tonight coming through Rocky Point."

He picked ten troopers and gave them their orders. They were lean, weathered men in all sorts of ragged uniforms, but they handled their horses and their carbines with the skill of long practice. The poor old mule was hard put to keep pace with their fast-stepping mounts.

It was not very long after noon when the cavalcade rode in through the plantation gate and past the deserted mansion to the tobacco barn. Anse hammered on the door.

"It's me—O'Neal," he called. "Got some friends here you'll be glad to see."

Tracy opened the door a crack and looked out. "By George!" he exclaimed. "Confederate cavalry! They *are* friends, sure enough!"

Two hours before, he explained, they had seen a couple of Yankee soldiers prowling around the empty stables. They had finally gone off southward. Apparently they had been stray foragers from the platoon Anse had met.

"I threw a scare into the main bunch of 'em," said Anse. "Reckon they wouldn't dare bother us anyhow with this escort. If you're ready, sir, we can hitch up an' make Rocky Point while it's still light."

All of them were tired of being cooped up, and the captain fully approved of moving on at once. Within twenty minutes the teams had been harnessed to the

wagons. With a cracking of whips, the procession moved
out to the highway.

Now that a couple of troopers had taken over the scout-
ing duty, Anse rode alongside the lead wagon. In spite of
the hardships of the journey, he found Lucy and her
mother in cheerful spirits.

"Why," said Mrs. Harcom, "by this time tomorrow we
may even be in Richmond!"

One of the men in the cavalry guard overheard her. "I'd
sho' hate to disappoint ye, Ma'am," he remarked, "but
the train gen'ally takes three days—if it's runnin', that is.
The Yanks cut the Weldon Railroad below Petersburg
more'n a month ago. On'y way ye kin git to Richmond
now is 'way 'round by way o' Raleigh."

The lady took the news calmly. "We'll just have to wait
and hope," she said. "I know General Lee realizes how
important it is to keep supplies coming from Wilmington."

"Reckon he does, Ma'am," the soldier admitted, and
they rode on in silence.

Lucy looked down at Anse and made a little face. "Is
your mule as comfortable to ride as he looks?" she asked.

He grinned back at her. "I know that seat's mighty
hard," he said, "but I doubt if you'd want to trade. His
back's awful sharp an' bony."

A little before four o'clock they passed over the brow of
the hill and saw the valley of the Cape Fear below. The
cavalry troop was still on guard at the bridge. As the
wagons approached, the officer rode out to meet them.

"Lieutenant Wilmot, Fourth Georgia Light Horse, at
your service, ladies." He bowed to Mrs. Harcom and Lucy,
then nodded to Tracy. "We've seen no Union troops, and
I'm sure the other side o' the river is clear. Wish I could
accompany you, but our orders are to hold this bridge.

You should have no trouble reaching Rocky Point. It's only a few miles ahead."

He gave Lucy a smile, which she returned prettily, and the wagons rumbled on across the plank bridge. Anse, riding in the lead, felt his hackles rise. In these last few days, he had come to think of the girl as if she somehow belonged to him.

Before the winter dusk fell, they plodded into a little town and saw the board railroad depot squatting beside the track. There seemed to be nobody on duty there, but when Anse peered through a dingy window, he saw an old man bent over a telegraph key. As it clicked, he was taking down the message. At last he rose and hobbled to the door.

"What's all this?" he asked peevishly, staring at the line of wagons.

"This," said Tracy in a tone of authority, "is a consignment of arms and ammunition for General Lee's army. Here's the shipping bill. When do you expect the next train north?"

The old fellow examined the papers Tracy handed him, peering through cracked spectacles. "Wal," he replied, "the train's done pulled out o' Wilmington. I jest got it on the wire. But he don't stop here 'less'n I flag him down."

"All right—do so," the captain ordered sharply. "This shipment's important. Also there are two ladies here who want tickets through to Richmond."

The station agent shook his head dubiously and started back to his telegraph instrument. "Can't stop a train 'thout I git permission from the division super," he grumbled.

The answer he got must have been satisfactory, for a moment later he picked up a red lantern and lighted it, then sold Mrs. Harcom her tickets.

Darkness was coming on, and the winter wind blew

cold beside the tracks. Anse took Lucy's hand and led her over to stand in the lee of the wagons. They were both very quiet, now that the time of parting was near.

She snuggled into the curve of his arm. "I suppose," she said, "we aren't likely to see each other again as long as the war lasts. What will you do now, Anse?"

"Whatever the skipper wants," he told her. "I'm afraid the *Gray Witch* is done for, though. If we have to leave her, I reckon I'll be going back to Ocracoke."

"If I wrote you a letter there, would you get it?" she asked.

"All depends. Mail isn't too reg'lar, even in peacetimes, but it would probably reach me some day. Where'll I write to you in Richmond?"

She gave him the address of their boarding house, and he memorized it. Then he felt her shiver and drew her closer to him.

"I don't think," she whispered, "that the South can hold out very much longer."

There were tears on her cheek, and he brushed them tenderly away. Then a locomotive whistle hooted, and down the track they saw a headlight glow. For a moment they held each other close in a farewell embrace.

In response to the frantic waving of the lantern, the engine slowed and ground to a halt with a swish of escaping steam. It took only a minute or two for Tracy to explain why the train had been flagged. Then a dozen soldiers who rode as guards were helping load the cases and barrels into an empty boxcar.

"All aboard!" shouted the conductor, and Lucy and her mother climbed the steps into the one coach. By the dim light of a kerosene lamp inside, Anse saw them sit down next to a window on the station side of the train. Then the engine chuffed into motion. With a heavy heart Anse waved good-by.

164

                              *   *   *

A few minutes after the little train had rattled off into
the night, the boy drivers prepared to take their wagons
back to the coast.

"We'd better go with 'em," Tracy told his pilot. "No
telling what's happened to the ship, and I've got to find
out."

Anse tied his mule to the tailboard and sat beside Tracy
on the wagon seat. As the cavalcade plodded off, the captain spoke thoughtfully.

"Whatever happens now," he said, "I reckon we've done
our best. There's mighty little chance o' taking the runner
to sea again, and no place to go if we could, but I'll see
what I can do for the crew. Then I must get to Charleston, one way or another."

Anse understood his anxiety about his mother. "Maybe
we can get some news in Wilmington," he said. "Find out
if Sherman's headed for Charleston. An' I'd sort o' like to
see Hobe Gaskill again. Do you figure we could go 'cross
country to Wilmington?"

"Don't know why not," said the captain. "I'll have to
go there anyhow if I head south."

He paused before he turned to Anse again. "That's a
dangerous trip the Harcom ladies are starting," he remarked. "A rough experience for a sixteen-year-old girl
like Miss Lucy. She and her mother are thoroughbreds,
though. They'll stand up to it. Am I wrong or do you
think quite a lot o' the girl?"

Anse felt his cheeks grow warm and was glad it was
dark. "I reckon I do," he answered soberly.

Eighteen

They traveled all night, sleeping by turns. After a brief stop for breakfast, they reached the village on the creek before noon. The *Gray Witch* was no longer at the pier. But the storekeeper assured them she was anchored somewhere down around the bend and that there had been no sound of gunfire from that direction.

Tracy and Anse hired a small skiff and set out to find her. Within an hour they were aboard the runner, being heartily greeted by Calhoun and the seamen. Then old Mac-Ivor, Donald Burns, and the stokers came hurrying on deck.

"We've had no trouble from the Yankees," the mate reported. "The gunboat that was lyin' off the bar took off last night. Only thing that's happened is a couple o' hands jumped ship. Got sick o' settin' around, I reckon, an' went off afoot to find a tavern."

Tracy chuckled. "Too bad they didn't wait to get paid off," he said. "I'd planned to give each of you the money that's due you and let you go. There's a little creek over yonder with high reeds growing along the banks. I figure we can beach the steamer in there, lower the stacks and masts so she can't be seen, and just leave her there."

MacIvor's face was lined with grief. "Aye!" He sighed bitterly. "An' what's to become of her puir bonny engines? They'll a' be rusted oot!"

The captain patted his shoulder and grinned. "Cover 'em all over with grease, Mac," he said. "You've got plenty of it, and it might as well be used. Grease the bearings, too. Who knows? Maybe the *Gray Witch*'ll run again some day."

They maneuvered the ship deep into the creek and left her hard aground in the mud, where the bulrushes screened her well. Then the cook gave them a final meal, cleaning out the galley. The men gathered their belongings and made preparations to depart. They had plenty of money, for Tracy paid each man in gold.

At least half of the crew were British subjects and had their papers to prove it. They would almost certainly find their way home eventually. The others, in the present unsettled state of the war, should be able to melt into the countryside without attracting too much notice.

Mike Rudge was in a different category. If anyone recognized him, he might be arrested as a U. S. Navy deserter. Tracy understood this and agreed to let him accompany Anse and himself as a sort of handy man.

Saying good-by to Donald Burns was hard for Anse, for they had become very good friends. But he knew the young engineer was homesick for his native land.

In the gathering dusk the ship's company rowed her boats up to the little fishing village and left them there as payment for the use of the wagons. Tracy had a word with the storekeeper before they departed, and Anse saw some money change hands. The captain was making sure someone would have an interest in guarding the steamer. Meanwhile, by twos and threes, the men of the *Gray Witch* drifted off into the dark.

When Tracy was ready, his own little party set off on foot. Anse and Rudge carried their sea bags and a few provisions. The skipper took nothing except a heavy satchel. They followed the same road over which the

cargo had been hauled and trudged along it for two hours
before turning off to the left, in the direction of Wilmington. Once, away to the south, they saw bivouac fires
burning.

"Probably Yankees," the captain said. "We'd better
keep well clear of 'em and stick to the woods."

Fortunately, there was enough moonlight filtering
through the pines to show them the way, but even so, their
progress was slow in the next few hours. Sometime before
dawn they lay down and slept on the matted pine needles.

It was broad day when Anse woke up. He smelled
coffee boiling and found Rudge getting breakfast. Tracy
had gone to a nearby hill for a look around. When he returned, he was whistling cheerfully.

"I know where we are," he said. "Wilmington's just
over yonder—not more'n an hour's walk. No sign of any
Union troops about, either."

There was misery in the town when they reached it. All
the newly rich people had fled when Fort Fisher was captured, and the poorer folk were out of work and half
starved. Tracy went to see the agent who had handled
shipments through the blockade, but the offices were
bare and empty. The man had taken his family and gone
off to Fayetteville. Dejected-looking Confederate soldiers
slouched along the deserted streets, waiting for the inevitable time when General Terry would decide to attack
Wilmington itself.

The spirits of the three men sank even lower when they
visited Mrs. Evans's rooming house. She told them tear-
fully that Hobe Gaskill was dead. The infection in his
lung had grown worse after Christmas, and he had finally
succumbed on the first day of the new year.

"There wasn't a thing the doctor could do to help him,"
she sobbed. "Poor man—at the last he would hardly taste
any food. Just got weaker and weaker and coughed all the

time. He left this for you," she told Anse. "Said he knew you'd take it to his sister on that outlandish island where he lived."

What she gave him was a tightly wrapped parcel, heavy in his hand. He nodded. "I'll see she gets it," he replied.

After that sad meeting there was little more to keep them in the city. They parted at the railroad station, where Tracy and Rudge hoped to take a train south. The captain gripped Anse's hand.

"Good luck to you, lad," he said. "I've a feeling you'll hear from me when the fighting's over."

"Thanks, sir," Anse replied. "We had some good voyages. I reckon you'll find me back at Ocracoke."

*   *   *

It was good to feel the bite of the sea wind on his face again and hold the straining sheet of a sailboat. He lay back in the stern, one arm on the tiller, and cruised north-eastward up the narrow sound.

Two days earlier he had walked the now familiar route from Wilmington to the little village above Topsail Inlet. There he spent the night and found an elderly fisherman who was willing to sell him a boat. It was a skiff, considerably smaller than the old *Goose* but trim and seaworthy, rigged with a leg-o'-mutton sail. In the city he had changed a hundred dollars of his gold into more than a peck of Confederate notes, and he used this paper money for board and lodging, provisions, and the purchase of the boat.

That wasn't all he had added to his possessions. Back in the woods, a mile from any house, an awkward hound puppy had come floundering after him through the brush. It was thin and bramble-scratched and footsore. And its great, brown, pleading eyes were too much for Anse. He gave the dog some of the bread and meat he had brought

169

to eat along the way, and from that moment the little fellow would not leave his side.

In the village he asked where the puppy belonged, but nobody knew. "I guess he's mine, then," he said with a laugh. "Come here, boy. I'm goin' to call you Rip."

Rip lay between his feet as he sailed. In color the dog was black and tan, with a white breast, white feet, and a white tail tip. Possibly a foxhound, Anse thought, though he might be part beagle. His ribs had filled out after a couple of good meals, and the scratches were healing well. On the long trip up the sounds, it was pleasant to have him for company. Animals were among the things he had missed aboard the blockade runners.

Between Topsail and New River Inlets, he saw a few fishing boats and talked to the men in them.

"Any Yank gunboats in the sounds?" he asked.

"Not so many now," he was told. "They don't bother small boats, anyhow. Reckon they figger the war's about over."

He did sight one Union war vessel as he sailed past the islands in New River Inlet, but the ship was anchored a mile away to the north and paid no attention to his skiff. Before dark that night, he had passed Brown's Inlet, Bear Inlet, and Bogue Inlet. By moonlight he put into a little creek on the shore of Bogue Sound and slept comfortably under a blanket and tarpaulin, with Rip snuggled against him.

He figured he had sailed sixty miles that first day. Unless he ran into head winds or bad weather, he might hope to reach Ocracoke in another forty-eight hours.

It was fine enough when he set out, but by noon the sky had darkened and the wind blew harder from the east, forcing him to tack. When the waves increased and the skiff began to take water, he had to beach her in a cove a few miles west of Beaufort Inlet. It was raining hard

now. He took his duffel and the dog and made his way through the wet sand to a group of fishermen's shacks that huddled in the dunes of Bogue Bank.

The few people there were whalers, waiting for the early spring run of whales. At the moment they had barely enough to eat, so they weren't especially friendly. However, they allowed him to bed down on the floor and keep the puppy with him. When the storm had blown itself out two days later, he was glad to pay them for their grudging hospitality and leave the island.

With a light land breeze abeam, he sailed past Fort Macon, now in Union hands. More gunboats were anchored off Beaufort and Harker's Island, but again they showed no interest in the little sailboat. By afternoon he had passed Shackleford Bank and was well up Core Sound, making good speed.

"Rip," he told the hound, "we're only fifty miles from

home. If the wind holds an' we get a good moon, what do you say we try to make it tonight?"

Rip's only answer was to beat a tattoo with his tail on the bottom of the boat and look up at his master with adoring eyes.

They passed Drum Inlet at sunset. Shortly after that the moon rose big and bright over Portsmouth Island, and the broad waters of Pamlico Sound opened up ahead. Anse had sailed them since he was a child, and he could have found his way blindfolded. It was ten o'clock when the skiff bounced in the tide rips of Ocracoke Inlet. Four or five miles farther on Anse steered in through a narrow channel, dropped anchor, and lowered his sail in the tiny circular harbor of Ocracoke Village. There were no lights in the houses ashore. He knew everybody had been in bed for hours, so he rolled up in his blanket and slept aboard once more.

It was Rip's cold nose touching his cheek that woke him a little after daybreak. Neither of them had eaten any supper, and the dog was hungry. Anse sat up, stretched, and looked at the familiar waterfront. The same boats he remembered were tied up at the same docks. Smoke was rising from the chimneys of houses he had known all his life. A man in seaboots and a jersey came clumping down the dock, tossed a bundle of nets into a skiff, and stood there staring at the new boat in the harbor.

Anse got up, laughing. "Howdy, Rufe!" he called. "How are they runnin'?"

The man on the pier nearly fell into the water in his astonishment. "Anse O'Neal!" he whooped. "Well, by gums! We figgered you was drowned or a pris'ner by now!"

Anse pulled up the anchor and sculled his boat rapidly to shore. By the time he tied up at the dock, half a dozen other villagers had gathered.

"Your folks know you're home?" asked Rufe Garrish.

"Whar'd you git the skiff?" Dud Styron inquired.

He climbed out and shook hands all around, answering their questions as best he could. Then, with willing helpers to carry his duffel, he tramped up the sandy street to his family's house. A few half-tame ponies, grazing on the roadside grass, snorted at the little hound. Anse climbed the step to the door, and before he could knock, his mother was there, holding out her arms.

After breakfast his first duty was to visit the house on the other side of the harbor where Sarah Gaskill lived. She heard the news of her brother's death quietly, saving her tears till Anse had left. The parcel he gave her contained a considerable sum in gold—all Hobe's savings.

When he came home, he spent the rest of the morning telling his family about his adventures. His father sat by with a proud look on his weather-seamed face, and the two little girls were wide-eyed and speechless. It was Mrs. O'Neal, bustling about the kitchen, who asked most of the questions.

"You shouldn't have sent us those expensive dress materials," she said. "Must have cost a month's pay. They're handsome, all right, but I'd rather you'd saved your money."

Anse laughed and unbuckled his heavy belt. "Heft that, Ma," he said. "It's gold—an' all mine. There's close to twenty-five-hundred dollars there."

The family was awe-struck. It was more money than anybody on the island had ever seen at one time.

"What you aim to do with it?" John O'Neal asked him.

"Keep it, I reckon. Might want to buy a bigger boat some day or build a house."

"A house, eh?" his mother put in. "You thinking o' getting married? Seems as if you must ha' met some girls on your travels."

Anse flushed under his tan. He found it hard to talk

about Lucy. "Reckon I'll stay single a spell," he told her.

After the noon meal he went out with his father in the old fishing boat. They sailed five miles up the sound and put out a net. Then they sat talking for an hour while the boat rocked on the swell. A pair of pelicans and a dozen white gulls flapped over, squawking as they waited hopefully for the net to be pulled. When it was brought into the boat, however, it held only seven or eight mullet—a typical winter catch. The birds took one look and flew away in disgust.

" 'Nough for a few meals," said Anse's father. "Won't begin to catch many 'fore May."

Back at home, Anse ate supper, then wandered over to the general store, where he knew some of his friends would be gathered. Dud Styron, Rufe Garrish, and Hank Midgett were there, along with his cousin, Joshua O'Neal. They sat around the potbellied stove and swapped yarns.

Josh had served aboard a Union blockade ship until he was wounded by a bursting cannon and invalided home. "Sure glad I got out when I did." He chuckled. "I might ha' been shootin' at my own kin if I'd been aboard this last fall."

"Not many gunners could hit the *Gray Witch*," Anse told him with a grin. "Too fast, an' our skipper was too slick. Well, I guess the gunboats won't have much to do now. Blockade running's dead enough with the Cape Fear inlets closed. Matter o' fact, I reckon the war can't last more'n another three months."

Cut off from things as they were, they laughed at this idea. After four years of it, the war seemed like a permanent institution. Even Anse had no way of knowing how true his prophecy would be.

Nineteen

For the most part, it was a quiet time he spent at home in Ocracoke. There was little to do there in winter. He cut some firewood, mended the fence in front of the house, patched the roof where shingles had blown out in a hurricane. When the weather was fair, he sometimes roped a pony and took long rides up the beach, where driftwood lay in tangled heaps and the skeletons of old wrecks took the battering of breakers on the shoals. Occasionally he helped his young sisters with their reading and writing.

In March the men of the village tarred their two whaleboats, sharpened the harpoons, and checked the long whale lines, coiling them down in the tubs. A lookout was kept on the outer beach from daylight till dark. He had a long pole with a white flag at the top, and if he sighted a spout, it was his duty to wave the flag as a signal.

One afternoon Anse heard an excited shout down the street. Dud Styron, waving wildly back and forth, was pointing eastward at a white speck. Within five minutes a dozen men, young and old, were racing to the beach. They launched the whaleboats through the surf and pulled mightily in the direction of a low white spout, a mile or more offshore. It vanished for minutes at a time, then reappeared not far from where it was first seen.

Anse had an oar in the first boat, manned by six stalwart islanders. His uncle, gray-haired Abel O'Neal, was steering, and forward, with his knee braced in the chock, Rufe Garrish held the harpoon ready. In ten minutes of hard rowing, they were "on the whale." The spout appeared only fifty yards away, and for a moment they saw the great dark back like a slowly moving island.

"Easy now," Abel O'Neal ordered. "He ain't seen us yet. Be ready when he blows again."

The other boat came alongside while they waited. The minutes seemed to drag. Then suddenly the water boiled, and right between the two boats the spout went up with a moaning roar. Garrish gripped the shaft, steadied himself, and hurled the harpoon deep into the black side of the monster. At almost the same instant, the harpooner in the other craft was fast to the whale.

"Starn oars!" Abel bellowed. " 'Ware flukes!"

The blades bit the water, and the boat backed off just in time. Glancing over his shoulder, Anse saw the vast tail flukes rise high in the air and come down with a tremendous crash that drenched the rowers. Then the whale sounded. The line went whistling out, and soon the first tub was empty, the second emptying fast. At last the line stopped uncoiling, and Rufe Garrish snubbed it quickly around the bow post. They waited less than a minute for the wounded beast to start its run, and when it came, they were suddenly snatched through the waves at frightening speed.

"Hang on, boys!" shouted Anse's uncle. "He's a big 'un but not too big. With two irons in him he can't go fur."

The double drag of the boats slowed the whale down before they were out of sight of land. For a minute or two the line hung slack, and Abel O'Neal used the interval to change places with Garrish. He had a long, sharp lance in his hand.

There came another upheaval in the sea, a hundred feet ahead. The whale breached, throwing itself half out of the water in a vain effort to shake loose. Then the rowers drove the boats close to the dark, gleaming sides, and the two lances went in almost at the same instant. In a welter of blood and a final thrash of flukes, the whale died.

It was a back-breaking job towing the huge carcass ashore, but the rowers were in a triumphant mood and made light of it. On the beach the women and children had been collecting dry firewood. Soon the flames were heating the big iron try-kettles. With sharp-edged knives and spades, the boat crews cut away the blubber in long strips, chopped it into pieces, and threw the dripping fat into the kettles. As it boiled, the oil was run off through straw-lined troughs into barrels.

This was a forty-barrel whale. In two days they had stripped away the blubber, cut out the baleen, or whalebone, from the head, and towed the rest of the carcass out to sea. Only the tongue had been taken for meat, and on the second night the villagers feasted on this famous whalers' delicacy. When the proceeds of the oil and whalebone were shared out, every family on the island would have money for provisions.

By the first of April, Anse was beginning to grow restless. Very little news had come to the island since his arrival, and there was no longer any regular mailboat. Early one morning he got into his skiff, taking Rip for company, and sailed off across the sound to Swan Quarter, forty miles northwest.

Although it was the county seat of Hyde County, Swan Quarter was an insignificant little town, and as he had expected, there was no Federal garrison there. He did catch up with the news, however. The Charleston forts had surrendered in February, and many of the city's warehouses and stores lay in ashes. Sherman was still moving north after destroying Columbia, and the reports were that he had reached Goldsboro, North Carolina, hardly more than a hundred miles away. Even worse, Sheridan's cavalry had crossed over from the Shenandoah to smash what was left of Jubal Early's army and move down to join Grant. When Lee made a desperation attack on the Union line in front of Petersburg, he had been driven back, and after that the Confederate Government started getting out of Richmond. Now, as the postmaster expressed it to Anse, it was "about all over but the shoutin'."

He got some lunch for himself and the young hound and started back shortly after noon. There was a southwest breeze that allowed him to reach without tacking, and he had time to think about what he had heard.

He wondered whether Ransome Tracy had been able to reach Charleston and if he had succeeded in taking his mother out of danger. It was saddening to think of the lovely old house at Fair Winds possibly burned or mutilated by Yankee soldiers. And even harder to bear was the thought that Lucy Harcom was probably still in the doomed capital of Richmond. If her father left with Lee's staff, the girl and her mother would hardly be taken along. He wished he had some way to go there and look after them.

Rip felt the distress in his master's mind and licked his hand, whining softly. It was dark when they sailed into the harbor at Ocracoke. Anse moored his boat and tramped heavily home.

The next day he discussed his news with the men and boys around the store. Almost all of them agreed that "Marse Robert" had little chance of breaking out of the Yankee trap.

"He's got to fight or give up," said Dud Styron. "An'

with four times as many men against him, he can't win any more. Them pore fellers o' his are starvin', too."

Anse nodded. "I heard they're mighty short o' food an' ammunition in Richmond," he said. "Lee may try to break away an' head west, but the Yanks'll be right on his heels. My guess is he'll surrender before he lets half his army get killed."

"Wal"—Rufe Garrish sighed—"I reckon secession jest never would work, anyhow. This was meant to be one country. It wasn't just the abolitionists—it was the rich folks with slaves that started the war."

Anse hated to admit it, for he had come to be a loyal Confederate, but he knew in his heart that it was true. They argued about what would happen after peace came. Some thought the North would make life miserable for all Rebels, military or civilian, but Josh O'Neal disagreed.

"Ol' Abe," he insisted, "wants to patch up the differences an' give Southern folks a chance to git back on their feet. Whatever you've heard about him, he's a good man. I seen him once, at Fortress Monroe."

"Anyhow," said Rufe Garrish, "it ain't likely to make much difference to us, out here on the Banks. 'Pears like we've got nothin' they can take away from us."

When he was in Swan Quarter, Anse had mailed a letter to Lucy Harcom at the address she had given him. Whether it would ever be delivered, he had no idea, but at least it gave him some comfort to write.

A week later there was a commotion on the island. One day about noon a small Union gunboat was sighted, half a mile off the harbor entrance. She appeared to be stuck on a sandbank. Josh O'Neal organized four or five men to sail out and try to help her, and Anse went with them. The tide had been low when the vessel started in, and she had missed the unmarked channel.

"You'll have enough water to back her off in another

hour or so," Josh called to the lieutenant in command. "Anything you want us to do?"

"Yes," he replied. "We've got a sack of mail for Ocracoke. But we've brought news, too. Lee surrendered to Grant at Appomattox Court House on the ninth of April. The war's over, boys."

After an astonished moment while the words sank in, the islanders raised a cheer.

"Hold on!" called the lieutenant. "Don't start whooping it up yet. Just a few nights later some crazy man shot President Lincoln when he was sitting in a theater. He died the morning o' the fifteenth. Everybody, North an' South, had better be sorry about that. He'd have made the peace a lot easier for you Rebs."

"Who are you callin' a Reb?" Josh asked angrily. "I fought in the U.S. Navy, just like you!"

They waited till the gunboat's paddles slid her off the shoal, then took the little mailbag back to the village. Anse was delighted to find that two of the letters were addressed to him. He opened the one from Richmond first.

"Dear Anse," Lucy wrote. "Perhaps you have heard the news of the surrender. Mamma and I were here when the Yankees came in. I must say they have been very fair and courteous, but before leaving, our own soldiers set fire to the warehouses where the cotton and other supplies were stored. Most of the city burned, including the house we were in. We got out into the street with just a few clothes and no money.

"During the fire some of the townspeople broke into stores of provisions and looted them. They made off with tons of hams, bacon, flour, and sugar and smashed barrels of whisky, lapping it up from the gutters. Anse, they were like animals!

"Yesterday, with the Union army in charge, we stood in

a long line of people, colored and white, and finally we were given a ration of hard bread, which is all any of us have to eat.

"We have heard from my father at Appomattox, and as soon as he can, he promises to come for us. We don't know what we'll find when we go back to Staunton or even just how we'll get there. Certainly we won't be rich now. But Daddy's wealth is in his brains. As a lawyer, he's sure he can make enough to keep us alive.

"If you receive this, dear Anse, we shall probably be gone from Richmond before you can reply. Some day come to Staunton if you can. I would be a very unhappy girl if I thought I was never to see you again. Ever yours, Lucy."

The other letter had been more than two months on the way. It was dated in Charleston, February 10, and was written in Ransome Tracy's bold, dashing hand.

"My dear O'Neal," it said. "Things are pretty hot here, as you may have heard. An attack is expected any moment, coming from both land and sea. I have at last persuaded my dear mother to come away with me, and we shall attempt it by carriage, since most of the railroad is now in Yankee hands. Where to go is a problem, but if the usual Tracy luck holds, I expect we shall find some safe haven.

"The way this war is going, it can't last much longer. When the smoke settles, I expect I'll find my feet on a deck once more. If so, I'll let you know. Mike Rudge sends his regards, as does 'Mis' Margaret.' All my best to you, boy—R. Tracy."

*   *   *

Spring came late that year on the wind-swept Outer Banks. Anse had put in his time digging a fine big kitchen garden for his mother, but the seeds didn't get a good start until the latter part of April. Then two weeks of hot weather brought them along with a rush. Peas, beans, and root vegetables were flourishing by early May. Anse guarded them from wandering ponies and from the cows and pigs that roamed freely through the village.

In the meantime, he went out several times with the fishing boats. His father welcomed his help with the nets, and as the spring advanced, their catches were heavier.

By mid-June, when the local fishermen had salted and dried all the fish they needed, it was decided they should send a boatload across to the mainland and try to sell them. Anse volunteered to be one of the crew. They took a big sloop, owned by the Garrish family, and set out at the crack of dawn one fine summer morning. In the hold they carried half a ton of salt fish, and on deck was a wooden tank containing fresh-caught shrimp. To keep them alive, they poured bucketfuls of sea water into the tank every few minutes.

A brisk northwest breeze filled the mainsail as they skirted the shoals and headed down Pamlico Sound to the west of Portsmouth Island. Soon they were in Core Sound. Before noon they made two stops at small Carteret County ports but found no market for their cargo. The people along these shores did their own fishing.

"Might as well keep on to Beaufort," Anse suggested. "We can make it into the harbor there 'fore dark."

The gunboats were gone from the channel now. At dusk the sloop rounded the point where Fort Macon's empty gun emplacements frowned and hove to in the roadstead off Beaufort. They slept aboard, keeping a deck watch to supply water for the still lively shrimp.

Anse was awake at daybreak. He watched a boat or two move out from the docks and saw laborers coming down to start the day's work. Soon a sound of hammering reached him from the shore. A little way above the town there was a small shipyard, and as he looked more closely, he could see a long, low steamer berthed there. Her sides were painted with red lead, and workmen were building a superstructure of some kind on her deck. But there was something about the vessel's lines that gave him a homesick feeling.

Anse called his cousin Josh and pointed to the ship. "Ever seen a steamer like that?" he asked. "Forget what they're doin' to her an' just look at her shape."

"Sure!" Josh exclaimed. "I'll be doggoned if she ain't a blockade runner!"

They heaved anchor and sailed the sloop along the waterfront till they found an empty space where they could tie up. A fish market near the docks was just opening for the day. Within half an hour, they had sold their shrimp for a fair price and their salt fish for a very low one. Then the little group of Ocracokers went to a restaurant for breakfast.

Anse was just finishing his second cup of coffee when he saw a familiar figure come in the door. The man was gray-whiskered, squat, and sturdy and walked with a sailor's rolling gait.

"Mike Rudge!" Anse cried as he leaped from his chair. "You old porpoise—where'd you come from?"

Twenty

Rudge was fully as surprised as Anse. "Is it really you, boy?" He chuckled. "Sho' never figgered to run into you here. Ye look like life's agreein' with you, too."

The boy introduced his old shipmate to the rest of the island crew, and Mike sat down and ordered breakfast.

"It's this way, Anse," he explained. "After the war ended an' things begun to settle down a mite, Tracy an' me come back to Topsail Inlet. The *Gray Witch* was still thar—rusted some but sound enough. We got a few hands together an' started her engines, an' after two days we managed to kedge her out o' the mud. Tracy'd made some sort of a dicker with the owners an' bought her cheap. So we sailed her up here to Beaufort, an' she's bein' refitted. The skipper's idee is to make a coastwise packet out of her an' go in business."

"Where's the cap'n now?" Anse asked.

"At the hotel—'less'n he's already over at the steamer, bossin' the job."

"Well, hurry up an' eat," Anse urged. "I want to go see him."

They found Tracy aboard the one-time runner. He was striding around the deck, handsome and cocky as ever. And he greeted Anse like a long-lost son.

"I'd have sent for you before long," he told the young pilot, "but I wanted to have her finished first. It'll be a couple more weeks before the passenger cabins are ready and the furnishings in. See this? A whole double line of 'em, from foremast to mizzen—twenty cabins in all. There'll be a regular enclosed bridge forward, with a better view ahead. And I plan to paint her white, with black trim."

His enthusiasm was catching. Anse could already picture her as a fine-looking ship, and he wanted tremendously to have a part in the enterprise.

"Got a pilot yet, sir?" he asked shyly.

Tracy laughed. "No," he said, "we'll have to use the regular harbor pilots because I want to make all the main ports from Norfolk to Savannah—maybe Jacksonville. But I'll need you, O'Neal. There's no telling where Calhoun's got to, and if you like the idea, I'd planned to sign you on as first mate. The pay won't be as good as it was running the blockade, but the work ought to be steady— and peaceful!"

Anse was flabbergasted. First mate! The offer was beyond anything he had dreamed of.

"Golly, sir!" he gasped. "That's wonderful. You can sure count on me!"

*　　*　　*

As soon as Anse came down out of the clouds again, he asked Tracy about his mother. The escape from Charleston by carriage had gone smoothly, with old Obed handling the reins. By back roads they had passed the invaders east and south of the city and in two days' driving had reached a sea island near the mouth of the Savannah River. There was a plantation there, owned by one of Tracy's brothers.

"A lot o' the field hands went whooping off with Sherman's army." The captain chuckled. "But now their master's home, most of 'em are back, working for wages.

Being free didn't turn out to be all they expected, I reckon."

Together they went over the steamer from stem to stern. The engines and boilers were in surprisingly good condition. Tracy explained that he had tried to contact MacIvor without success.

"But I had a piece of luck," he said. "Got a letter from Donald Burns. The lad's still in Halifax, and I think he'll come down here to be my engineer. I remember you got on well with him, and he seems to know his engines."

The news pleased Anse. "That's great!" he said. "When will you be needing me, sir?"

"The work on the ship won't be finished for several weeks," Tracy replied. "I'm going to change her name, by the way. *Gray Witch* doesn't sound quite right for a passenger packet. Thought I might call her the *Lucy*. How's that strike you?"

Anse could see the mischievous twinkle in the skipper's eye, but he couldn't help blushing. "I reckon that's a mighty pretty name," he mumbled, then changed the subject. "Would it suit you, Cap'n, if I went off for a little trip an' came back here after the first o' July?"

Tracy nodded. "I'm sure we won't have her in commission before then," he said. "You might try recruiting a few more men for the crew. These Ocracokers seem to make good hands."

Anse promised to see what he could do and went back to the sloop. That afternoon they started their trip home. When he told his news to the other fishermen, two of them volunteered at once for crew duty on the new packet. They were youngsters like himself, with no families to support and an urge to see the world. But he knew they were good seamen.

Three days after they reached the island, Anse was preparing for another trip. Now that he had the promise of a steady job, he felt he could spend some of his savings with a clear conscience, and the thing he wanted above all was to visit Staunton.

He sailed his skiff across Pamlico Sound and up the Neuse River to New Bern. There he took a train to Goldsboro, changing to one that ran to Richmond. The railroads had been repaired after a fashion, and while few trains ran on time, they were at least back in service.

He had a few hours in the old Confederate capital before starting west. Up to that time little had been done to rebuild the burned and ruined city. Many of the houses were charred shells, and the people on the streets looked dispirited and underfed. Even the summer green of trees couldn't take away the blighted look of the once beautiful town. Anse was glad to get away from it and board an evening train headed for the Shenandoah country.

When he woke, early the next morning, they had left Charlottesville and were climbing a twisting grade through the foothills. He rubbed his eyes and stared, for he had never seen mountains before. Ahead, the shaggy ramparts of the Blue Ridge seemed to blot out half the sky.

A few hours later the train was in the Shenandoah Valley and nearing Staunton. As the conductor called the station, Anse took his sea bag from the overhead rack. It

was the only kind of traveling luggage he possessed, but
it held his suit of good clothes and some fresh linen. He
slung it over his shoulder and walked along the street
till he found a hotel a short distance from the depot.
There he secured a room, washed off the railroad grime,
changed, and came down for breakfast.

There were several loud-voiced Yankee carpetbaggers
in the dining room, but he was lucky enough to get a
table by himself. He asked the venerable colored waiter
if he knew where the law office of Colonel Henry Harcom
might be found.

"Yas, *suh!*" answered the Negro. "Cunnel Harcom's a
fine man. He's right up the street, three blocks f'om here."

Anse found the office sign, mounted a flight of stairs,
and knocked at the door. A pale young law student
showed him in and went to the inner office to announce
him.

The colonel was a lean, erect man with smiling eyes
and prematurely gray hair. His empty right sleeve was
neatly pinned up out of the way, but with his left hand
he offered Anse a firm, friendly grip.

"Mr. O'Neal," he said. "I've heard so much about you,
it seems as if we were well acquainted. I confess, though,
it's a surprise to see you here, so far from the seacoast.
What brings you to Staunton?"

"I reckon you've already guessed, sir," said Anse with
a grin. "If you don't object, I'd like to call on your
daughter."

The lawyer had a twinkle in his eye, but he spoke
gravely. "Before I give you my unqualified approval," he
replied, "I'd like to know a little more about you. Your
prospects, for instance. You can understand how precious
Lucy is to us."

"Yes, sir," said Anse. "As far as prospects go, I think
you'd call 'em pretty good. Captain Tracy's refitting our

old steamer and starting a packet line. He's asked me to be his first mate. If we make a go of it an' add more ships, I reckon I may be in command o' one of 'em before too long. Anyhow, I'm going to study up for my master's license. I don't plan to stay an Ocracoke fisherman."

"Good!" said the colonel heartily. "That's the spirit that'll put the South back on its feet. At the moment I have no appointments. Why don't we walk up to the house and see the ladies?"

The Harcom home turned out to be a large brick structure with white stone steps and pillars flanking the doorway. The lawn and gardens, Anse could see, had been neglected for lack of servants. But the place must have been really imposing in the days before the war.

As they reached the door, it suddenly opened and Lucy appeared. She must have come straight from the kitchen, for her face was flushed, and she was wiping floury hands on her apron. At the sight of Anse over her father's shoulder, she let out a little cry of dismay.

"Come in!" She laughed. "But don't look at me till I've run upstairs and tidied myself. Mamma'll be right here."

No sooner had the girl gone than Mrs. Harcom came into the hall, as poised and gracious as Anse remembered her. She greeted her husband, then held out both hands to the young visitor.

"These days of peace seem to have agreed with you, Anse," she said. "You're so tanned and so tall! A young man now, and a very handsome one!"

She was as pleased as he could wish when she heard his news. "Captain Tracy's a very fine and understanding man," she said. "He did a great deal for the South in the war, and he seems ready to help in these hard new times of reconstruction."

Then Lucy came racing down the stairs. Without a

moment's hesitation she flung her arms around Anse and kissed him hard. Then she stood back and looked at him admiringly.

"I've got to put my cake in the oven," she said with a laugh. "Then we'll take a walk, and I'll show you the pretty parts of town."

*　*　*

They had a great deal to talk about as they strolled along the shaded streets. Lucy shuddered a little when she spoke of the last wretched days in Richmond, but she was so happy over the news Anse had to tell her that she soon forgot.

"First mate of the steamer *Lucy!*" she cried. "Why, Anse, you'll be well off—making enough money to—" She broke off then, blushing with embarrassment.

Gently Anse took her hand. "Yes?" he prompted. "Enough to get married on, I reckon you meant to say. Well, it's true. Your folks wouldn't want me to rush things, but ever since I first saw you come aboard the *Gray Witch,* I've never thought about any other girl. I couldn't say so before, but—well—would you wait for me —marry me some day?"

"Oh, Anse," she said, "you goose—don't you know I've loved you for perfect ages? The answer's yes!" And for the second time that day he was firmly kissed, right in broad daylight and in the middle of the brick sidewalk.